DEVIL GUN

by

STEVE PICKERING

Published by New Generation Publishing in 2020

First Edition

Paperback ISBN: 978-1-80031-929-5
Hardback ISBN: 978-1-80031-928-8

www.newgeneration-publishing.com

New Generation Publishing

I dedicate this book to my loving wife Kathleen:

My two sons, Shane and David, and my beautiful
daughter Suzan.

And all of my lovely grandchildren :-
McKenzie: Tyler: Grace: Scarlett: Mylie: Olivia:
George:

Contents

Chapter 1

Man o' War

On the twentieth day of September, 1846, Denim Armstrong reached the age of twelve. Living on his father's farm near Portsmouth Docks, England, he worked hard, feeding the livestock and cleaning out the pigsties. Every morning at the crack of dawn he began his chores in the barn, where the grain was stored. After filling two large buckets with swill, he would hook them onto the wooden yoke that he placed over his shoulders and struggle up a steep gradient to the pig enclosures. Many times a day would he make this short journey, to feed more than one hundred voracious animals with their daily rations. This manual work structured his young body and made him strong and muscular. With broad shoulders and sturdy legs, he looked much older than his dozen years.

Every time he started up the hill to the sties, he would whistle his favourite sea shanty and listen to the clamour as the swine jostled for prime position at the feeding troughs. Denim was convinced the pigs recognized the tune; they always knew when he was coming.

Upon reaching the summit for the umpteenth time that September day, the burden across his shoulders became heavy. Resting both buckets on the ground, Denim took a breather. He shoved locks of brown hair out of his eyes and mopped his sweating forehead. Catching his breath, he emptied the remnants of the swill and watched the animals clamber over one another, grunting and fighting, trying to get inside the meal trough as though they had never been fed. Their antics never failed to amuse him. As he kneed the flanks of the pigs, so he could exit the pens, they squealed even louder. 'With all that noise, anyone would think you were being slaughtered.' He always spoke aloud to the animals as if they understood. Pleased to have finished his daily stint, Denim strolled down the hill to the barn. Cleaning the swill tackle and putting it away, he washed himself down and locked the large double doors. Making his way across the cobbled courtyard to the limestone cottage, he glanced at the giant silver birch towering above the apple trees. It had been a few years since he and his two older brothers had climbed to the top, or had even played in the orchard.

He lifted the latch on the weathered door of the farmhouse and entered. Mother, all five-foot-two of her, round and cuddly, stood at the scullery table, making dinner.

'Is that you, Den?' she shouted, without turning.

'Yes,' he replied. The smell of cooking reached his nostrils. Since he was a little boy, he had often helped his mother to bake.

'Can you take the peelings out to the pigs?'

'But Ma, I've only just finished feeding the pigs,' he grumbled.

'Now then my boy, we'll have none of that.'

Grabbing the overfull waste bucket, Denim marched back up the hill to the enclosures. When he returned, fresh bread in baking tins had been pulled out of the oven. He was about to sneak a crust when a large wooden spoon rattled across his knuckles. 'No you don't! Your father will be home in another hour, and we will all eat together.'

Denim did not mind the reprimand, for he knew

his mother doted on him. Whenever he was chastised by his father, mother always saved him from a beating. Although strict, his father was a caring man too, and Denim would not have swapped his parents for any others, and he knew that his two elder brothers and his younger sister felt the same.

An hour later, the family was sitting at a sturdy oak table in the dining room. Sunlight through an open window highlighted the bur-reed mat that covered the floor. Above the mantelpiece over the log fire, a sizeable portrait of grandparents looked down as father recited a thanksgiving prayer. In the strictest of silence, they dined on homemade rye bread and broth, followed by pork stew and dumplings. Only when father had finished eating were the two eldest sons allowed to leave the table. Told to remain seated, Denim watched his young sister trail mother into the scullery.

Preening his bushy moustache, father pushed away from the table and pulled his favourite pipe from a wooden rack on the mantelpiece. Standing with his back against the fireplace, he delivered his news in a puff of smoke. 'I saw Sean O'Reilly today, down by the dockside. I told him how you are always going on about a life at sea. And he told me, one of his men is leaving his employ to go work in London, and that would leave a position for a new starter on his fishing boat. It's long hours, mind, and a man-sized job, but I do believe you're up to it. What do you say, son?'

Denim's real passion was to work on one of the large naval ships that came into port but, not wanting to displease father, and thinking that once he had gained experience on the fishing boat he might more easily obtain work on one of the galleons, he agreed.

'That's great news, Father – when do I start?'

'Well, according to O'Reilly, in about seven days' time.'

'As soon as that! But who will take care of the pigs?' Denim had become quite attached to the animals.

'Don't worry about them, your two brothers will share that chore, along with working the land.'

'Should I go and see Mr O'Reilly?'

'No need for that, son,' said father, waving his pipe. 'I thought you would be interested, so I told O'Reilly that you would take the job.'

After thanking his father, Denim left the room. It would be another year before he would be allowed to enlist in the Royal Navy, but working on the fishing boat now was exciting. He could not wait for the week to pass.

Next day, after completing all his farmyard chores, Denim walked two miles into town and sat at the dockside. The harbour was his favourite place to idle. He loved to watch the ever-changing scenery as trawlers, river barges, merchant boats, and many ships from other countries came into port. But now an extra thrill accompanied those pleasures, for in a few days' time he would be working on O'Reilly's fishing boat.

Daydreaming that he was captain of a warship, Denim threw stones into the water and imagined cannon fire. Smiling, he remembered his younger years at the harbour, playing pirates with the other boys that lived near the port, and how he had soon become their leader because he was smarter and stronger than them. But those memories faded fast when he caught sight of the British Royal Navy ship sailing into port. The busy harbour never failed to enchant him, yet to see a mighty man o' war was the greatest thrill of all. With flags flying high above huge canvas sails, and the crow's nest at the top of the mainmast, it dominated the harbour majestically. *Endurance* was the nameplate on the bow. He had not seen the ship before.

Denim's excitement peaked when the captain appeared on the quarterdeck. Against the red uniforms of the marines, the dark-blue jacket stood out; gold braid at the shoulders and brass buttons gleamed in the afternoon sun. Plumes of white feathers were displayed on his tricorn hat, while the long cutlass hanging from a gold sash around his waist declared him as the High Commander of the warship.

There was always a chance of cannon fire practice from one of the ninety guns that protruded from the perimeters of the ship, and Denim was not disappointed. The master gunner shouted 'Fire!' A thunderous roar from the cannon saw a huge cascade of water spout into the air, as the cannon ball crashed into the sea. Although Denim had watched the procedure many times over the years, it still enthralled him. Inspired by colourful stories of life at sea, as told by the old sea dogs who reminisced on the quayside, Denim dreamt of the day when he would become captain of the most impressive of warships. Lost in thought, little did he realize how soon his daydreams would turn into a nightmare of reality.

Chapter 2

Lessons Learned

On his last working day on the farm, Denim told the pigs that he was going out to sea and that, although he would not be there every day, he would still get to see them from time to time, albeit weeks apart. He knew the pigs were ignorant to everything he said, but still, it made him feel better. After slapping the animals' rumps in a fond farewell, he joined the farm workers who had invited him to the local tavern to celebrate the new job.

Business merchants, farm workers, navvies, and pedlars all made merry in the overcrowded room of the Smugglers Inn. Customers' pipe smoke, trapped by the low-beamed ceilings, fogged the Georgian windows and made Denim's eyes smart. Feeling tipsy, he had stayed longer than he had intended. He was about to leave the cheerful atmosphere when he saw a small boy weave his way through the noisy crowd to a man who was worse for drink, and whisper in his ear. Rising from his seat, the man followed the boy outside. Minutes later, the boy reappeared and approached a second man. A message given through cupped hands compelled that man to leave. This sequence of events repeated until four men had left the inn, and no one seemed to notice, or care, that they did not return. When the boy approached a fifth victim, Denim's curiosity got the better of him and he followed.

Taking deep breaths of fresh air to rid the smoke from his lungs, he looked upon the deserted street. A full moon highlighted the sea mist as it swirled in from the harbour and up the cobblestones towards the inn. Far off in the night, a dog barked its loneliness. With no one in sight, Denim was about to go back inside the inn when the boy emerged from a hidden alleyway. On seeing Denim, the boy dashed back into the darkness.

'Hey! Wait!' Denim shouted, and gave chase. Running down the alleyway, he lost sight of the boy but came across a horse and cart. Loud groans made him peek under the canvas covering. Drunken men were piled high. Suddenly, shadows moved on either side. A bag dropped over his face and a bang on the head rendered him unconscious.

Denim awoke on a wooden floor strewn with straw. He felt the large bump on his head, and recalled the shadows in the alleyway. A small lantern on a water cask gave a dim view of his prison. Low beamed ceiling, wooden walls with horizontal struts every three feet, and an arched door. Between him and the exit lay a score of inert bodies. Rats scurried out of sight as he stood upright. Carefully, he stepped over the drunken men and tried the door. Finding it locked, he retraced his steps and waited on the bed of straw.

As the other prisoners began to rouse, it soon became evident that they had all been kidnapped by press gangs. The young boy had lured the men outside the inn by implying that a loved one or someone of importance was waiting. Clubbed unconscious, the men were thrown in the cart and transported to a ship. According to the elders, there would be no chance of escape and they would all live the rest of their days as slaves on the high seas.

When the prisoners were brought onto top deck, they

realized they were far out at sea, without a strip of land in sight. To Denim's amazement, he found he was on the *Endurance*, the very same ship that he had been admiring in the harbour only a few days previously.

Pushed along in a queue by red-uniformed marines, he was surprised how many men had been taken prisoner. Young, old, fat, slim, well dressed or ragged – the press gangs had not been discriminate in their choices. Several men became seasick and were taken to sick bay; the rest of the prisoners were forced to sign the ship's ledger as proof that they had voluntarily enlisted in the Royal Navy. Many could neither read nor write, but their mark or scrawl was accepted. Those that refused were dragged to the cells below the ratline.

'Without grub in their bellies, it won't be long afore they're begging to sign the book,' scowled the scruffy mariner who was dishing out food to the captives

'Aye, unless the rats don't get them first,' scoffed the mariner's mate.

After signing the ship's ledger, Denim moved along the queue to receive one scoop from the water barrel with a pewter mug, a dollop of burgoo on a square wooden plate, and one ship's biscuit. He sat with the other prisoners on the deck and, when they had all eaten, they were ushered, single file, down a stairwell to meet the chief bursar. Hammocks and kitbags were issued, and each man was shown his space in the sleeping quarters. Taken back to top deck they faced a tall, muscular black man.

'It's the bosun,' whispered one of the prisoners.

Old sea dogs on Portsmouth Docks had told Denim how brutal the bosuns could be. Naked to the waist, with dreadlocks of hair touching his shoulders, this bosun looked fearsome as he delegated the men into work gangs.

Denim was polishing brass handrails around the perimeters of the ship with brick dust, when one of the prisoners refused to work. He watched with horror as the bosun beat the man unconscious with a steel belaying pin and dragged him away. Whenever the bosun was around, Denim worked more vigorously.

The following day, while swabbing the decks, he saw marines lay seven dead men out on the boards. Stripped of all clothing, their bodies were thrown into the sea. He recognized three as the prisoners who had been struck by seasickness.

Life on board ship did not get any easier for Denim. Work was tedious and repetitive, but he did not dare idle for fear of the bosun; a man who was unpredictable and violent. Anyone foolhardy enough to resist his demands was beaten and incarcerated in the cells below. Even more terrifying were stories that he often threw slackers overboard to feed the sharks.

These accounts terrified Denim and his worst nightmare was to face the bosun's anger. However, long hours of monotonous labour, and lack of sleep due to falling out of the hammock at night, made him lethargic during the day. One morning, while buffering the safety rails, he dozed. A friendly sailor named Pegs awakened him with a dour warning to stay more alert but, unable to keep his eyes open any longer, Denim rolled under the captain's barge.

An excruciating pain in his right ear awakened him. He was about to scream out, but when he realized it was the bosun who was twisting him by the ear, he dared not make a sound.

'So you're tired, are you, my little hearty?' snarled

the bosun. 'Let's see if this wakes you up!' Pulling Denim by the ear he hurled him face-first into the mainmast. Blood poured from Denim's nose.

'Now, let's see how tired you are.' He yanked Denim's head back by the hair. 'You're going way up there, on lookout duty.' He pointed to the highest reaches of the topgallant-mast. Denim could see the small platform of the crow's nest.

'You take a nap up there my little hearty, and you'll be falling to your grave.' He shoved Denim against the mast. 'Now get climbing, and if you're still alive in three days, I might let you come down.'

'Three days! How will I get food?' A punch in the head sent Denim sagging onto the mast.

'Don't answer back,' growled the bosun. 'Now get aloft, before I throw you overboard. Go on, get going!' He gave Denim a hefty kick up the backside.

Glad to escape the bosun's clutches, Denim climbed the mast. Every step higher, the wind blew harder. He had always been a good climber of trees on the farm, but ascending the mast while the ship rolled and pitched proved difficult, and more than once he lost his footing. Out of breath, he scrambled onto the five-foot-square platform. He could see the bosun watching, a hundred feet below.

Standing upright Denim grabbed the safety rope circling the crow's nest. Flags on the mainmast whip cracked like gunshots as strong gusts of wind tried to blow him off the perch. All day he scanned the horizon for hazards; storms, pirate ships, or land. When night descended, he hunkered down on the platform to sleep. As he did so, he spotted a lone figure climbing up the rigging. His heart raced in fear. Was it the bosun?

'Here you are, laddie,' a voice shouted. 'I've

brought you some water.' Relieved to see the friendly sailor, Denim guzzled from the leather pouch.

'Hey! Take it steady with the water, laddie,' said Pegs. 'I don't know when I'll be able to get back with more. The bosun's been watching me like a hawk lately, but I'll see you tomorrow if possible.'

Denim watched as Pegs descended the rigging like an agile ape and disappeared through a hatch on the main deck. With one hand holding onto the safety rope, Denim tried to sleep, but every hour he was disturbed by the night watch as they did their rounds of the ship. At five hundred hours, the bugler's raucous reveille sounded, and men ran from all corners of the ship to line up for morning inspection. The master-at-arms deployed the men to their duties and the ship continued its journey.

Two hours later, the bosun's mate piped breakfast. As Denim watched the crew going to the galleys to feast, he drank the last drop of water from the pouch and wondered if he would survive another day without food.

Late in the afternoon, Pegs appeared with fresh water and a small portion of skate wrapped in a piece of sailcloth. While Denim ate the fish, Pegs made a simple hat out of the cloth.

'Put this on,' said Pegs, 'it will help protect you from the sun. Now, I'd better get back to my job. If the bosun finds out I'm feeding you, he'll have us both walking the plank.' After gliding down the rigging, he again disappeared through the hatch.

As Denim scanned the horizon, squawking gannets, following in the ship's wake, waited for the jettison of the daily refuse. Several black dorsal fins popped out of the sea as a school of pilot whales splashed to the surface and then disappeared into the depths. Further out, he spotted a pod of bottlenose dolphins as they regrouped and playfully swam away. With no land in sight, the sea looked endless.

It was a long day and, with nowhere to hide from the mid-day heat, he was pleased when the fiery red sun dipped into the sea and the cool breeze of evening gave him some respite. As the ship coasted across moon-illuminated waters, stern lanterns were lit and sails furled, and all activity on board ceased. Lulled by the gentle motion of the sailing vessel, Denim's hand slipped off the safety rope. In deep slumber he slumped across the platform.

Skies darkened and winds gathered momentum. Torrents of rain stung Denim's face. Pushed high on rising swells, the ship suddenly dropped into a deep trough. With eyes opened wide, he slid across the rain-soaked platform. A fumbled grab for the safety rope caused him to plummet thirty feet, until his foot caught on the loose rigging. Swinging upside-down, the wind and rain slammed him hard against the mast. Denim wrestled to free his foot and swarmed up the pole. Pulling himself onto the crow's nest, he hung on for dear life.

Early morning sunshine aroused Denim's cold body from sleep. As he stood upright to view the calm seas, gut-wrenching pains doubled him over. Clutching at his belly, he choked and heaved as yellow bile spewed from his mouth. He remembered the men who had died of seasickness. What a horrible death they must have suffered.

A hundred feet below, the ship was bustling with activity as the crew began their daily chores. Storm lanterns were extinguished, sails were unfurled, and the ship surged forward. Relieved of watch duty by one of the crew, Denim descended the rigging and vowed never again to let the bosun catch him sleeping. Pleased to get his feet back on the deck, he heard breakfast piped. Collecting his food in the mess, he sat alongside Pegs at a trestle table. As he bit into a biscuit, he gave a loud shriek and spat it out. A brown beetle scurried out of the crumbs and ran across the boards.

'Ugh!' he exclaimed and crushed the bug underfoot.

Pegs laughed aloud. 'You'll soon get used to eating them, laddie.'

'Never,' said Denim, disgusted at the thought.

Pegs gave another hearty laugh. 'Save the biscuit until nightfall, laddie. You enjoy the weevils much better when you don't see them.'

'You're jesting,' said Denim, unsure of his new friend's humour.

'No,' said Pegs. 'All the old hands wait until the lights are out before eating their biscuit. On these long voyages the oats become infested, but you can't afford to refuse any food. If you do, you're likely to catch scurvy.' Unsure if Pegs was pulling his leg or not, Denim saved the remaining part of the biscuit until nightfall when he was in the hammock.

Assigned to kitchen duties the next day, Denim whistled his favourite sea shanty while carrying pans of prepared vegetables from the mess to the galley cooks. The tune reminded him of the pigs back at home, but his nostalgia was cut short when Pegs appeared from nowhere and nudged him to one side.

'I wouldn't whistle if I were you, laddie. Not on board this ship, anyways.'

'And why not?'

'Only the galley cooks are allowed to whistle on board this ship.'

'Why is that?'

'Because, while ever the galley cook can be heard whistling, the men know he can't be spitting into their food.' Denim started to laugh, but stopped short when he saw Pegs' face was without a smile.

'The men believe whistling on board ship brings bad luck and, hearing you, one of them might take umbrage and come slit your throat.' Pegs left Denim to ponder the remark.

Uncertain as to whether Pegs had been joking, and even though he thought he had caught sight of a wink, he never whistled again. Denim was grateful to his wirily built friend, who he guessed was in his late thirties. Straight brown hair and a thin bony face did not lend much in the way of good looks, but compared to the motley individuals on board this ship, Pegs was handsome. And without his help, Denim could see that life at sea was going to hold many dangers. As their friendship grew, Denim confided in Pegs, who responded by talking about his own life; how his parents had died of consumption when he was very young, and how he had been locked away in a workhouse, until escaping and enlisting in the navy.

Denim became reliant on Pegs' knowledge and companionship and, as the weeks and months passed, he adapted to the sailors' way of life, even mastering the hammock by not falling out of it. On days when life became more challenging, he would think of his family and friends, and pine for the day when he could return home.

During the crew's free time on the forecastle, he would sit at his favourite spot near the bowsprit and revel in the wonders of the sea: porpoises, marlins, flying fish, and the variety of birds – sea eagles, puffins, petrels, and cormorants. Sea life was never-ending, and every part of the ocean that the ship traversed brought some new delight: enormous shoals of jellyfish, squid, and his first sighting of the giant turtle as it swam on its endless journey.

In the evenings he would gaze in awe at spectacular sunsets on the horizon: blazing reds, striking pinks, and rich purples. Staring at the turquoise waters, he would often become hypnotized in thought, and would wish that life on board could be as blissful as his daydreaming.

Chapter 3

Blackie

Moving from one task to another, Denim quickly gained the skills of seamanship, but he had not liked any of the jobs he had been assigned to, until he was sent to the sailmaker. He ended up mending sails alongside a tall, skinny boy who had a slight speech impediment. Denim was amazed when he discovered Jack was from Portsmouth.

'Y-You were lucky, living on a farm,' said Jack. 'We lived in the slums, and because of my f-f-father's illness, and with two younger brothers and th-three sisters, I became the breadwinner. I had to clean chimneys on rich people's houses. The dirty work gave me this b-b-bad chest.' He gave a whistling cough and banged his chest several times to endorse the statement.

'Three years ago I was s-sh-shanghaied and t-tossed onto this ship. I was the cabin boy, but the captain couldn't put up with my bad habit, so I was sent here. The sailmaker doesn't s-say much, but he's all right.'

Denim confided to Jack his fears of the bosun. 'Bosuns don't last long on this ship,' said Jack. 'The crew ch-chopped the last one up with a meat cleaver, and threw him overboard.' A cold shudder ran through Denim. What else was in store on his dream ship?

One morning, while Denim was stitching sails using a sailmaker's palm, the needle snapped and two inches of fine steel became embedded in his wrist. The sailmaker gave permission for Jack to take Denim to sick bay. After moving along corridors and stairwells, they came to a long room. A blood-stained table, lit up by two oil lamps, showed a daunting array of instruments: saws, pincers, scalpels, lances, needles, and a mallet. On several shelves above were displayed medicine bottles containing coloured lotions.

Three men occupying makeshift beds were receiving medical attention, but when the surgeon saw the two boys, he came over and cared for Denim's injury. Swabbing the wound with vinegar, he withdrew the broken needle with tweezers, and then applied a bandage. Denim thanked the surgeon and followed Jack out of the room.

On the return journey, they came across two men who were removing a wooden panel from the passage wall to take out a barrel of wine. Quickly, Jack pushed Denim down an alternative route and together they made haste back to the sailmaker.

Out of breath, Jack flopped down on a pile of sails. 'I hope they d-d-didn't see us.'

Denim wondered what all the fuss was about. 'Who are they?'

'It was P-P-Patch, and Gr-Grimes.'

'Patch and Grimes?' Denim queried.

Jack had a coughing spasm before he could answer. 'Grimes is a pickpocket and a thief, and n-n-nothing is safe that his fingers can touch. The one with the black eye cover is Patch. They say he lost an eye while f-fighting pirates in the Caribbean. He's very dangerous. The type that would s-s-slit your throat while talking to you.'

'But why are you so scared of them?'

'They're Blackie's gang and they was pinching the

ship's liquor.'

'Blackie? Who is Blackie?'

Jack nearly fell off the pile of sails. 'W-What! You don't know who Blackie is? Everyone's scared of Blackie, and no one dares to cross him.' Denim wondered why no one had warned him of a man that everyone else onboard ship was afraid of.

'Blackie works in the pumphouse, below the waterline,' said Jack. 'Food is taken to him daily, by one of his l-l-lackeys. They say he sleeps down there, but no one seems to know exactly where. And he has a nasty habit of appearing, in the unlikeliest of places. No one knows the ship's secret p-passageways better than Blackie.'

'What does he look like?' Denim asked.

'Oh, you'll know him all right when you see him. He's the biggest man on board sh-ship. A large black ring on his finger bears the skull and crossbones. Story is, he won the ring in a cutlass fight by ch-chopping the man's finger off.' Leaning closer, as if he was about to divulge some terrible secret, Jack whispered, 'The most striking thing about Blackie is the t-t-tattoo on…' His words suddenly tailed off when the sailmaker appeared with a fresh bundle of sails to be mended.

Jack waited until the sailmaker had gone, but instead of finishing the description of Blackie's tattoo, he ended the conversation with a shake of his head and a grim warning. 'It's safer to see nothing and s-s-say nothing on board this ship. You n-never know who might be listening.'

No matter how hard Denim pressed to find out more, Jack refused to say anything else.

That night Denim found it difficult to sleep. But the

snoring men, in rows of hammocks surrounding him, were not to blame. Instead, the gruesome pictures of Blackie that his mind conjured up kept him awake until after midnight.

Out of the dark, steel-like fingers gripped Denim's throat. He shouted in terror as a giant shadow lifted him out of the hammock. Through the swirling darkness he was carried to the top deck. Strong hands dangled him over the taffrail. He could see the violent waves crashing below. What was happening? Who was trying to kill him? He screamed for help, but roars of the raging sea drowned him out. Skull and crossbones glowed from a large black ring. Demonic laughter echoed all around. Then he was falling topsy-turvy through the air. Plunging into the cold waters, he swam frantically to the surface. The ship was leaving him behind. He grabbed a long rope trailing from the stern. Three knots, seven knots, and then twelve, the ship pulled him through the pounding waves. Suddenly, a tremendous water spout lifted him forty feet into the air. Then he was floundering in the sea. Whirlpools dragged him down, into the depths. From a black void, huge yellow eyes gleamed. Long tentacles reached out and encircled him. The monster reeled him in. Its red beak of a mouth opened wide. Dagger-like teeth closed all around him.

'Aargh!' Denim sat bolt upright in the hammock. Lathered in sweat, his heart beat fast. He gave a deep sigh of relief, and glanced at the sleeping sailors. No one had heard his shouts. Lying back, he tried to sleep, but every time he closed his eyes the terrible nightmare returned. Then, in the distant night, he thought he heard a cry for help. He held his breath to listen. Only the creaking timbers of the ship and snores of drunken men came to his ears. Had he imagined the cry for help? Unable to sleep, he slid out of bed and quietly weaved his way between the rows of hammocks. Would Jack be awake? he wondered.

Jack had been in a deep sleep when a cold piece of steel had pressed hard under his chin. He had shouted for help, but a quick hand over his mouth had muffled the sound.

'Keep your mouth shut, boy,' whispered Grimes. Wide eyed, Jack nodded his head. 'If you snitch about what you saw today, you're a goner. Isn't that right, Patch?' Patch pressed the stiletto harder. Blood trickled down Jack's neck.

As Denim entered the quarters, he saw Patch and Grimes and the knife held at Jack's throat. Instantly, Denim charged. Both men were bowled over and Jack fell out of the hammock. Two marines, on night duty, came to check the sleeping quarters. Patch and Grimes scrambled on their knees and escaped via another exit. Jack jumped back into the hammock and pretended to be asleep. While Denim crept quietly between the rows of sleeping sailors, and without being seen, made his way back to his own quarters.

Climbing into the hammock, Denim thought how lucky he had been. Moving about the ship at night was a flogging offence. He lay there thinking about Patch and Grimes, but it was not long before morning reveille sounded. Dressing into his work togs, he found Pegs in the mess room and related the whole story.

'You've made two deadly enemies there, laddie,' warned Pegs as he ate breakfast. 'You'd best keep watch at all times now, or you're likely to end up with a knife in your back.'

Worried about reprisals, Denim asked, 'What if I told the captain who the wine thieves were?'

'Forget about that, laddie,' said Pegs assertively. 'If the crew got wind of your snitching, you'd be smiling from ear to ear.'

Denim understood the threat of having his throat cut, and decided against snitching. 'But what would happen to Patch and Grimes if the captain did find out?'

Pegs washed the last crumbs of hard tack down with a mouthful of grog. 'Pilfering the ship's stocks warrants the cat o' nine tails but, knowing this captain, he'd probably hang them. Their best chance of survival would be their leader.'

'Blackie? But how could he save them?'

'Well… for a long time now, the crew have suspected Blackie of being an informer. Whenever there was talk of conspiracy, the captain always found out in advance, and many a man has lost his life for even thinking about mutiny.'

'Then why don't the crew do something about Blackie?' asked Denim.

'Because they're afraid to,' said Pegs. 'If anything untoward should happen to Blackie, the captain might act out an evil revenge on the crew. Proof has been offered many times that Blackie is responsible for murders on board ship, but the captain has never brought him to book.'

Curious to know more, Denim asked, 'Who is Blackie and where is he from?'

'It's well known,' said Pegs, 'that Blackie had been on the run for many a year until he was arrested for murder on the back streets of London. To save his neck from the noose, he chose amnesty that imprisoned him on board this ship. Knowing he would never escape, he formed this gang of cut-throats that constantly rob and intimidate the crew.'

'I've been on board the ship a few months now – why I haven't seen Blackie?'

'Don't worry,' said Pegs, 'you'll be seeing him soon. Especially now you've met his two staunchest allies.' Denim gulped. The prospect of meeting a man that everyone was afraid of was frightening. 'And here's another piece of advice,' added Pegs. 'You'd better keep a lookout for Razvan, the Romanian gypsy. He's another one of Blackie's treacherous lap dogs.'

'How will I know him?'

'Huh, you'll smell him coming,' said Pegs, getting up to leave. 'The gypsy once survived a bout of scurvy, and his teeth turned black.'

Putting aside the grisly thought of Razvan's teeth, Denim made short work of the burgoo and then returned to the sailmaker. Jack was eager to give his account of the night's event, but before he could finish, the bosun appeared and beckoned Denim to follow.

Denim trailed the bosun down several flights of steps before he was suddenly shoved inside a room and the door banged shut. A solitary lantern gave him a dim view of the pumphouse and four chain pumps that siphoned bilge water from the hold. Silently, a powerfully built man emerged from the shadows.

Naked to the waist and arms folded, he stood there like a giant fairground wrestler. A striking tattoo of a hooded cobra covered his dome-like bald head. There was no mistaking the warning burned onto his forehead, the branding iron scar – letter P: *Prisoner, beware!* From a large black ring on his finger, the skull and crossbones glowed and Denim knew he was now in the presence of the formidable Blackie.

'Who stole the captain's wine?' The deep voice echoed across the pumphouse. Being alone with Blackie, in this poorly lit room, was more terrifying than the nightmare. Denim was speechless.

'Speak up!' boomed the voice. Trembling in fear, Denim tried to think of something to say.

'It'll be worse for you boy, if you don't speak up.' Blackie took one step forward. Denim almost ran to the door. 'I don't know who stole the wine,' he spluttered.

Deathly silence reigned before the voice growled, 'You'd better keep it that way, boy... or else!' As the words died out, Blackie was gone. For a while, Denim stood there, shaking involuntarily. Then, blowing a huge sigh of relief, he opened the door.

'Follow me,' said the bosun. With a lantern in each hand, he led the way into the very bowels of the ship, where hundreds of bags filled with shale lay in disarray. He ordered Denim to level the ballast and, with the second lantern showing him the way, the bosun retreated into the darkness.

Denim began work immediately; he knew the ship was always in danger of sinking if the ballast was not evenly distributed, but working alone with only a feeble light was eerie. The creaking timbers of the ship as it laboured against the sea sounded like wailing groans of the dead. Sometimes a loud crack would make him jump in fright and look nervously about.

He was pleased when, hours later, two crewmen came to take over the task. As he made his way back to daylight, he came across Pegs repairing fishing nets and recounted the meeting with Blackie.

'Blackie has met you sooner than I expected,' said

Pegs. 'I wonder why?' He pondered awhile, then said, 'Go check your kitbag, laddie, and make sure there's nothing amiss.'

As Denim entered the sleeping quarters, he bumped into a sailor who was making a hurried exit. Denim apologized, but the small man just cursed and quickly scurried away. A pungent smell made Denim think of Razvan. Searching through the kitbag, he was amazed to find a sparkling necklace. With the jewellery safely inside his pocket, he dashed back to the sailmaker, lest the bosun should be waiting for him. On arrival, Jack was missing and the sailmaker had no idea where the boy had gone.

Working alone made the afternoon long, but when the belfry bell rang eighteen hundred hours, Denim set out to look for Jack. A search of the sleeping quarters, sick bay, and the mess room proved fruitless. Gangs of sailors playing shake bones and dice on the forecastle said they had not seen anything of him. Spotting Pegs sunning by the bowsprit, Denim informed him that Jack was missing and told him about the jewellery and Razvan.

'Give me the necklace, laddie.' Pegs guessed that the gypsy had planted it. 'I'll sort this little matter out.' Denim handed the jewellery over, and then asked about Jack.

'He'll turn up,' said Pegs, as he laid back against the bowsprit in the sunshine.

Knowing he would not get any more out of Pegs now, Denim went to collect the hammock from the storage net. He suspended the bed from the ceiling rafters in the sleeping quarters and climbed into it. Humping bags of shale all morning had been tiring; he would find Jack tomorrow.

Chapter 4

The Gauntlet

'All hands ahoy!'

'Up hammocks!'

Awakened by the bosun's call, Denim realized he had overslept. Eyes barely open, he tumbled out of the swinging bed and got dressed. Sailors were in a flurry of activity as they readied themselves for morning inspection. Hammocks were rolled into bundles and chucked into storage nets as the men made their way for rota call.

Arriving at his place of work, Denim was greeted with bad news.

'Jack's locked in the cells below,' said the unsmiling sailmaker.

'Why? What's he done?'

The sailmaker ignored the question. 'The bosun's looking for you, and he's waiting in the sick bay.'

A shudder of fear made Denim queasy. He did not like to think the bosun was looking for him at any time. In sick bay, he found out that a sailor had died of typhus. Several more men had been moved to top deck and hosed down with seawater to get rid of body lice infestations. Given the task of cleaning, Denim scrubbed the walls and floors with holystone. As he worked, he worried about Jack. Had jewellery been planted in his belongings too?

Hours later, he heard an officer shout, 'All hands on top deck!' Pleased to down tools, Denim joined five hundred and more shipmates under the huge canvas sails. Curious to see what was happening, he wormed his way to the quarterdeck rails.

As the captain came out of the cabin, Denim thought how old he looked. His weathered face, with its hawk-like nose and cruel, grey eyes, was fringed by a silver wig that curled below his tricorn hat. Dressed in a blue uniform jacket, his white breeches gartered at the kneecaps over white stockings, highlighted his spindly legs and made him look top-heavy. He had an air of superiority as he sat at a folding table. On either side of him stood the first officer, and Lieutenant Thorpe.

Above this jury of three men, six marines armed with muskets, and a drummer, stood to attention on the poop deck. Drum roll sounded and the gathering quietened. Lieutenant Thorpe shouted for the prisoner to be brought to the fore. Grimes, face bloodied and bruised, was forced to kneel in front of the captain and the charges were read aloud.

'Theft of wine is a crime against the Crown,' proclaimed the first officer, 'and warrants punishment of the highest order.'

Grimes begged for mercy, but with little formality the captain pronounced him guilty of treason. A loud cheer erupted from the crew as they heard the verdict. Hanging for wrongdoers was always an excitement in their humdrum lives.

While Grimes was dragged to the mizzenmast, Lieutenant Thorpe shouted for the next prisoner. Expecting it to be Patch, Denim was surprised to see Razvan manhandled to the front. But he was even more surprised when the first officer held the sparkling necklace high as evidence, and accused Razvan of robbing the captain's treasure trove.

'Fifty lashes,' shouted the captain. 'Take him away!'

Protesting his innocence, Razvan was dragged

across the boards and shackled to the mainmast. When the last offender was called for, and Jack was thrown in front of the captain, Denim's knee's almost gave way.

'Thieving from one's shipmates is the most contemptible of crimes,' said the first officer, as he showed a handful of trinkets, rings, and coins. Jack stammered his denials, but a glancing blow from a marine's musket left him flat out on the deck.

Suddenly, the crowds began to chant. 'Sailor's justice! We want sailor's justice!'

At first, Denim thought the men were shouting support, but then he realized they were baying for Jack's blood. Fearful lest anyone should point a finger at him, Denim withdrew from the quarter deck railings and melted deep into the crowd. As the chants became deafening, Captain Bain looked down with contempt at the ill-bred crew. Although he scorned them, he sometimes gave into their rants as a means of appeasing rebellions against his authority. The gavel hammered down on the table. 'Sailor's justice it is, then,' shouted the captain. 'Take him below.'

Triumphant roars filled the air as Jack was dragged away. Then all eyes turned to the mainmast as Razvan's shirt was ripped off his back. The cat o' nine tails was shaken loose and the bosun began the flogging. Each lash of the whip bit deep into Razvan's flesh.

The excited watchers trumpeted the count: 'One! Two! Three!'

At thirty strokes, Razvan's knees began to buckle.

'Thirty-eight! Thirty-nine!'

His back flayed to the bone, Razvan slid down the pole and slumped to the deck. Unshackled, he was poured onto a stretcher and taken to sick bay. The crowds spilled over to the mizzenmast to watch the hanging. Pushed along by the horde, Denim could see Grimes struggling against the guards. With his hands tied behind his back, a noose was dropped over his head. A dozen men tugged on the rope hanging from the yardarm and Grimes sailed into the air. The rope tightened around his neck. His screams became muffled. His tongue protruded and his eyes popped. Mocking laughter from the crowds filled the air as Grimes kicked wildly. When the body became still, Lieutenant Thorpe and the other officers ordered the crew back to their duties.

Wandering gannets, sensing a meal, winged in from the heavens and lined up on the yardarms. When one hungry scavenger dared to attack, the rest of the flock swooped onto the cadaver, squawking and fighting for pieces of warm flesh.

Sickened by the sight of his first hanging, Denim could not believe how the men had delighted in such a gruesome death. As he made his way back to the cleaning job in sick bay, he came across Pegs on hands and knees, scrubbing hammocks.

'I didn't see you at the trial,' said Denim.

'Nope, I've seen it all before,' said Pegs, without looking up.

'They caught Razvan with the necklace. He was flogged.'

Pegs looked up and winked. 'That's what he deserved, laddie, isn't it?'

Denim smiled. The wink confirmed his suspicion that Pegs had planted the necklace in Razvan's belongings.

'Pegs... what is sailor's justice?'

'Why do you ask, laddie?'

'That's what the crew demanded for Jack's

punishment.'

Seeing that his young friend was distraught, Pegs started to explain. 'When six bells toll tomorrow morning, Jack will have to run the gauntlet and...'

'Run the gauntlet? What does that mean?'

'You'd better get down here, laddie, and help me scrub,' said Pegs, 'If the bosun catches you not working, he's likely to clap you in irons.'

Denim got down on all fours and began to scrub. Pegs resumed. 'Any man that's grieved about their keepsakes being pilfered can take part in sailor's justice. Jack will be forced to run between two lines of men, while they strike at him with whips.'

'Will he survive?'

'Most men do, but…'

The implications of 'but' sounded ominous to Denim. 'But! But what?'

'Well... It depends on who's at the end of the gauntlet. The last man can make Jack go back down the line.'

'Who's the last man?'

'Usually it's the bosun.'

'The bosun!' exclaimed Denim. 'He's the worst man to be at the end of the line. Why doesn't the captain choose the last man?'

'The captain never attends. He leaves it to the crew. Don't forget, laddie, this is the men's justice, and it's against one of their own kind.'

'But Jack's innocent. The stolen goods must have been planted by Razvan. Jack's not a thief. The men must know that, so why punish him? And how has Patch got away with it? *He* was involved in stealing the wine.'

'Blackie might have made a pact with the captain,' suggested Pegs. 'Grimes is hanged as an example to the crew and, perhaps, Jack is punished to deter snitchers.'

'But why would Blackie hand over Grimes instead of Patch?'

'Patch is an expert with a knife,' said Pegs, 'and he would kill anyone for his leader. Perhaps on this occasion his usefulness outweighed that of Grimes.'

'If the rest of the crew know what's going on, then why are they still going to punish Jack?'

Pegs made no comment.

'Has anyone ever survived two runs down the gauntlet?' asked Denim.

To Pegs' knowledge, no one ever had, but he did not want to worry his young friend. 'Let's wait and see what happens tomorrow, laddie. Right now, you'd better get back to your own job before the bosun finds out you're missing.'

Worrying for Jack's life, Denim went back to the mundane task of cleaning sick bay.

Next day, Denim awoke in an anxious state of mind. Thoughts of Jack running the gauntlet had disturbed his sleep. When he saw the men gathering their laundry, ready to be cleaned, he realized it was washday. With an assortment of clothes he joined them and began to scrub. It would soon be time for the bosun's inspection.

At eleven hundred hours, the belfry bell sounded six times. Several crewmen stopped what they were doing and left for the upper deck. Denim followed. At the aft of the ship he joined Pegs and thirty-six crewmen. The bosun formed them into two lines and gave each man a length of black hemp. Halfway down the gauntlet, Patch was knotting two pieces of hemp together, but when Denim saw Blackie at the end of the line, he cursed aloud.

Pegs grabbed Denim's arm to quieten him. 'Shh,' he whispered, 'And remember, you must be seen to strike out. Any man that doesn't will be forced to run the gauntlet.'

With their black whips at the ready, the men shouted with glee as Jack was brought onto top deck, naked and shivering, and pushed into the gauntlet.

'Run, you dirty dog, run!' screamed the bosun.

Missing with their strikes, Pegs and Denim watched Jack run by. At a pace, Jack tried to dodge the lashes, but telling blows made him howl in pain. Flecks of blood sprayed the air as black hemp criss-crossed his naked body. Protecting his face, he charged between the human walls. Reaching halfway, he tried to sprint by Patch, but a long piece of hemp whizzed around his neck, pulling tight. Jack dropped to the floor. Lashes galore cut into his flesh as he scrambled to his feet and ran on. A sailor stuck a leg out. Jack tripped and skidded onto his knees.

'Get him! Get him!' chanted the men.

Strikes rained down from all directions. Struggling to his feet, he staggered down the line. Whippings became fiercer. Lurching from side to side, he fell flat out in front of Blackie. The shouting stopped as the men waited to see what Blackie would do. In their silence, an albatross gave a loud squawk as it flew over the ship. Wind whistled through the canvas sails, and the thunder of waves pounded the bow as two muscular arms lifted Jack upright.

'Are you all right, matey?' Blackie spoke, as if caring.

Knees skinned to the bone, and quivering in shock, Jack could barely stand. From a multitude of cuts blood trickled down his white, naked body. Tears rolled down his gaunt face as he stammered for mercy. But before his words were formed, the muscular arms slung him back into the gauntlet.

'Run, you mangy dog, run,' Blackie shrieked.

Barging into the wall of men, Jack tried to escape the torture. Stinging lashes drove him back. Forced onward, he stumbled down the line. A long piece of hemp whistled around his head. He gave a brain-piercing scream and rolled to the floor. Blood poured from his eye.

Like a man possessed, Patch jumped to the fore, and thrashed Jack's huddled form. Instantly, Denim ran and dived on top of Jack, to shield him from the beating. Taken by surprise, Patch stood back. The men watched as Blackie came down the line and hovered over the two lads.

'So you think you have saved your friend,' snarled Blackie. 'Now you're going to take his place.' He stooped to grab hold of Denim.

'Hold it!' a voice boomed.

All the men turned to see who had shouted out, but when they saw Pegs shoving his way down the line, they were not surprised. He was the only man on board ship who dared to oppose Blackie.

Blackie's lips curled with menace as he pointed a finger at the boy. 'He's stopped sailor's justice. Now it's his turn to run the gauntlet. That's the rules.'

'You've had your pound of flesh for today, Blackie,' said Pegs. 'Leave the lads alone.'

When Blackie made a sudden grab for Denim, Pegs blocked the move. The two men squared up and eyeballed each other. Blackie knew that Pegs was an excellent bare-knuckle fighter; he had seen him dispose of many adversaries over the years. He had always avoided taking him on, but when he saw Patch pull the ebony-handled stiletto from its sheath and move stealthily behind Pegs, he grinned. It was time to get rid of his old foe once and for all. 'Get out of the way, Pegs, or you're a dead man!'

Pegs stood his ground. Patch moved in for the kill.

'Stop! Stop!' Lieutenant Thorpe came running from the stairwell, waving a pistol. 'Stop this nonsense at once, I tell you.' Although this was his first voyage on the *Endurance*, Lieutenant Thorpe had learned in that short time that Pegs was one of the most trusted sailors on board ship, and his friendship with the marines was well noted. On the other hand, Blackie was the scourge of the seas, and he would have shot him dead right there; but knowing that the man was in league with the captain, he dared not.

As the men closed ranks in support of Blackie, the lieutenant pointed the pistol. 'I'm warning you. Back off, or else!'

One by one the men threw down their whips and went back to their work posts. Patch took umbrage to Lieutenant Thorpe's interference and wanted to kill him, but with the pistol pointing in his direction he slid the knife out of sight and retreated, along with Blackie. A stretcher was shouted for and Jack was carried down to sick bay.

Thanking the lieutenant, Pegs nodded in the direction of Denim. 'It will be even more dangerous for the laddie now. Blackie doesn't like being beaten.'

'Then move the boy into your quarters, Pegs. You have my permission,' said the lieutenant, as he disappeared down the stairwell.

'You'd better go move your kit then, laddie,' said Pegs, 'or you're likely to wake up one morning with a dagger in your back.'

'What about Jack? Do you think he will be all

right?'

'I reckon so,' said Pegs. 'This surgeon's more learned than the last one. The crew poisoned him with his own medicine.'

'Will Jack lose his eyesight?'

'Questions, questions,' sighed Pegs. 'Let's wait and see what tomorrow brings, laddie.'

Denim had already learned that when Pegs became quiet, that was the last you would get out of him, so he gave up on the questions and went to move his kit.

As soon as it was morning, Denim went down to sick bay to visit Jack. All he found was Razvan, heavily bandaged and asleep. So the gypsy had survived the flogging, thought Denim. But where was Jack? He spotted the ship's surgeon, busy writing medical notes at a small desk, and asked him.

Without looking up, the surgeon replied, 'Oh, he died during the night.'

'What!' Denim gasped in shock.

Seeing how distressed Denim was by the news, the surgeon explained. 'Nothing could be done. I had to remove his eye. The trauma was too much. His heart gave out and he died – he wasn't a strong boy, by any means.'

Denim fought back the tears. 'Where's the body?'

'Bottom of the sea by now, I should think,' said the surgeon, 'Along with Grimes. We cut him down from the yardarm last night, and threw both bodies overboard.'

Nausea made Denim run from sick bay. On top deck, he leaned over the railings and vomited into the sea. Poor Jack – what a miserable life he had lived. Tears rolled down Denim's cheeks, but his anguish soon turned to anger and then to thoughts of revenge, as he pondered all the ways he could kill Captain Bain, Blackie, and Patch.

From that day on his character changed, from the homely farm boy that he had been, to a hardened victim of life at sea. He despised everyone on board ship except Pegs, who was the only true friend he had left; the man who, since the first day he had stepped foot on the *Endurance*, had protected him from the most fiendish gang of villains that had ever sailed the seven seas.

Over the coming months, he often thought how heartless the rest of the crew had been towards poor Jack. But life had to go on, and he was just thankful that he had Pegs' support. As their friendship grew, Pegs taught him many nautical skills: how to navigate by the stars, climb the masts and yardarms to secure the sails, and all the many types of sailors' knots necessary to tie down the rigging. With Pegs' tutoring, and his own eagerness to learn, Denim became an exceptional seaman.

During the long days at sea, he witnessed many disputes that often led to the death of one (or more) shipmate. Take what you want, when you want, was the order of the day among the sea dogs that manned this vessel, and he soon realized he would not survive long unless he proved to the crew that he was strong and capable. He had Pegs teach him the art of boxing and how to fight with a knife – the latter being a necessity, as most mariners carried a cut-throat and not one would think twice about using it.

Chapter 5

Fight to the Death

Over the years, as the *Endurance* patrolled trade routes to the Indies and chased pirate ships in the Caribbean, Denim matured into a powerfully built young man. All those years of carrying pigswill up the hill to the enclosures had made him very strong and now, at the age of twenty-five, he was capable of standing his ground against any man on board ship, including the notorious Blackie.

Denim's intellect and fighting ability were way above the average mariner, and although the rest of the crew were wary of him, they respected him too and, just like Pegs, he became popular among the marines. On occasion they would encourage him to arm-wrestle their champion, Isaac the German, but much to the chagrin of those who goaded him, they would lose their wagers as Denim often won.

One summer evening, after entertaining the marines, Denim retreated to his favourite spot and sat at the heel of the bowsprit. As the ship speared its way through the blue waters, fine sea spray moistened his shoulder-length hair and cooled him from the sticky heat of the day. He thought about his life at sea and how childhood expectations had not been realized. In these later years, he had often thought of escape, but opportunities had been few.

As he watched the flying fish skip over the water's surface, he began to reminisce: he imagined running down the green hillside from the enclosures of the pigsties; climbing the tall silver birch in the orchard; and the smells of home cooking from the farmhouse, where his mother and father, and the rest of the family, were waiting to welcome him. This blissful reverie was brought to an end when a chill wind made him shiver. He looked at the sky. Heavy clouds were gathering; it was time to go inside.

Making his way across the main gun deck, he came across Pegs, surrounded by Blackie and his gang. A loud argument had erupted: Pegs had accused Blackie of stealing a gold locket. Denim knew about the loose floorboard under the hammock, where Pegs' keepsakes were hidden in a trinket box, but he doubted anyone else did.

'Empty your purse, Blackie,' demanded Pegs. 'I want the locket back, now!'

'My purse stays where it is,' growled Blackie, as he held onto the small velvet bag fastened to the sash around his waist.

Suddenly, with both fists flying, Pegs lunged. One punch landed squarely on Blackie's jaw and rocked him backwards. Before he could retaliate, a left jab spurted blood from his nose. Like a raging bull, Blackie rushed at his attacker. Another series of blows stopped him dead. With fists held high, the two fighters circled. Blackie made a sudden charge. Sidestepping, Pegs delivered a vicious right cross that ripped open Blackie's brow. Roars of glee arose from the growing crowd of spectators.

With blood streaming down his face, Blackie sprang forward. But a solid right to the jaw sent him staggering backwards and spitting more blood. Wind-milling his fists, he rushed at his opponent. Pegs parried the blows and threw a salvo of punches that skinned Blackie's cheeks to the bone. The crowd went wild with excitement.

Not used to losing, Blackie began to fall back. This

pugilistic bombardment was sapping his strength; against such a skilful boxer, he was at a loss. He knew he needed to wrestle Pegs to the floor. Wiping the blood away from swollen eyes Blackie made one last, desperate attempt to catch his adversary. Arms open wide, he dashed forward.

The crowd gasped in astonishment as a devastating uppercut from Pegs dropped Blackie to his knees. As Pegs ran forward to deliver the winning blow, Razvan kicked over a cask of whale oil and flooded the arena. Slipping on the oil slick, Pegs fell headlong into two powerful arms that clamped tight behind his back.

Blackie gave a triumphant roar. His zest for the fight was renewed. Holding Pegs in a bear hug, he struggled to his feet. The advantage was his now, and he would not let go until Pegs had breathed his last. He summoned up all the reserves he could muster, for one final squeeze that would snap Pegs' spine in two.

Like a rag doll held in a deadly embrace, Pegs' face drained of colour. His head drooped and his arms dropped by his side. Suddenly, the storm clouds released their load. Torrential rain bounced off the boards. Deafening thunder claps reverberated across the ocean. Lightning ripped open the gloomy dark skies and lit up the whole deck. In those few seconds, as night became day, Pegs stiffened and slammed his head into Blackie's face.

Blackie's grasp was broken. He crashed to the floor. The ship rolled on the crest of a wave and sent him skidding, on his back, across the sodden deck. Hitting the base of the mast, he just lay there, barely conscious; face beaten to a pulp.

Opening the purse on Blackie's waistband, Pegs held the gold locket high for all the men to see. He smiled at the chorus of 'bravoes' as he crossed the deck towards Denim. Abruptly his footsteps faltered. His eyes opened wide in shock. Blood spewed from his mouth. Denim ran to catch Pegs' falling body. Embedded in his back was the ebony-handled stiletto.

With insane anger Denim glared at Patch, and then at Blackie sat propped against the mast. As the rain coursed down Blackie's battered face, his bloody lips gave way to a smile – a treacherous smile that said, 'I have won.' In his hand was the sheath to the stiletto.

Denim sprang at him like a wild animal. But all his attempts to reach Blackie were blocked by the gang.

As the rain abated, troops of marines came running. With bayonets fixed, they surrounded the horde and made a gangway for the captain. Striding pompously across the deck, he stopped in front of Blackie and then turned to the men. 'What have we here, then?'

No one answered.

'So the cat's got your tongues, has it?' Captain Bain was not used to being ignored. 'If someone doesn't speak up, and quickly, I'll have every man Jack of you whipped.'

Silence stilled the crowd.

Blood on Denim's face and clothes gave him away as the culprit. Captain Bain pointed a finger. 'Guards! Chain him to the foremast, we'll see if the cat can't loosen his tongue.'

As two guards grabbed hold of Denim, the downpour became heavy again. Deciding to take refuge inside the cabin, Captain Bain left command of the ship to Lieutenant Thorpe.

Patch had always hated the lieutenant for taking sides with Pegs and Denim many years ago. And bearing a grudge, he was reluctant to move when the lieutenant ordered him to throw Pegs' body overboard.

Lieutenant Thorpe was aware of the ill will towards him, so when he saw Patch's unwillingness to follow orders, he struck him across the face with a pistol. Bleeding from the cheekbone, Patch was forced at bayonet point to lift the body over the railings. As he did so, he pulled the stiletto out of Pegs' back and threw it at the lieutenant.

In that same instant, Denim pulled free from the two guards and dived at the lieutenant, and brought him to the floor. The stiletto hit a storm lantern and fell to the deck. Patch was clubbed unconscious and shackled to the grating on mid deck, and while Lieutenant Thorpe was helped back to his feet the two guards seized Denim.

Suddenly the ship was shrouded in a dense sea mist. Darts of blue flame flickered up and down the rigging and across the sails, until the entire contours of the ship pulsated with an eerie glow. Men shouted that the ship was on fire, but when their own bodies began to emanate the blue aura, their cries turned to panic. Running aimlessly about the decks they yelled, 'The ship is doomed,' and 'We're all going to die!' Trying to escape the strange firelights, some men jumped into the sea.

Hearing the commotion, Captain Bain came out of the cabin and onto the quarterdeck. 'Saint Elmo's fire,' he muttered in surprise. He had seen the strange lights many years ago, and he knew that they were harmless. 'Stand your ground, you fools. Stand your ground!' he shouted to the crew. But his commands were drowned out by the bedlam.

Frightened for their own lives, the two guards let go of Denim and tried to douse the blue aura on their bodies. Denim spotted the stiletto which had been washed closer by the rain. He ran across the deck and grabbed the knife. Diving full length he plunged the steel blade deep into Blackie's heart. A scream of death filled the air. Blood pumped down Blackie's bare chest. Knocked out cold by a marine, Denim was dragged to the cells below.

As the ship sailed out of the mist, the pulsating lights faded and the rain stopped. While terrified men were being pulled out of the sea, Razvan covertly pulled the stiletto out of Blackie's chest before the body was disposed of.

Leaving a skeleton crew on night duty Lieutenant Thorpe made his way to the wardroom, where the officers slept. He saw something sparkling on the deck. Picking up the gold locket and chain, he put it in his pocket for safe keeping.

Chapter 6

Keelhauled

Hours later, manacled and imprisoned behind a solid oak door, Denim awoke in the ship's hold. He nursed the bump at the back of his head and recalled the storm and the strange lights. Then, with a feeling like an arrow piercing his heart, he remembered that Pegs was dead. He tried to console himself with the knowledge that he had avenged his dear friend, and that by now Blackie was lying at the bottom of the sea.

Keys turned in the door. Isaac the German entered with a tray of fruit, hard tack, burgoo, and a small pewter of neat rum.

'I never knew prisoners were fed so well,' said Denim.

'It's not looking good for you,' said Isaac. 'When a full meal is given to a prisoner this early in the morning, usually they are hanged.'

Denim almost choked. 'What! For killing a blackguard like Blackie? The ship's well shut of him.'

'I agree,' said Isaac, 'but the captain has lost his greatest ally, and he's very angry that you killed him.'

'What about Patch? What's happened to him?'

'He was to be marooned, but with no chartered islands in the vicinity, they pushed him out to sea on a small boat.'

'But he could reach land.' Denim was angered to think that Patch might survive.

'Not without oars, food, or water,' Isaac smirked. 'He'll end up taking his own life with the gun.'

'What!' Denim nearly choked again. 'He's been given a gun?'

'One shot,' said Isaac. 'It's only humane, that he can take his own life.'

'It's too good for that scoundrel,' scowled Denim, wishing all the time that he had been put on the boat with Patch. His eyes gleamed at the thought of killing him.

'Don't worry, Denim, Patch will either blow his brains out or slit his throat with the knife.'

'Huh! So, he's been given a knife as well. If they are going to hang me, then I would rather have taken my chances on the boat. At least I would have settled an old score before I died.'

Seeing how strongly Denim disliked the man, Isaac explained. 'When Lieutenant Thorpe found Razvan in possession of the stiletto, he made him toss it onto the boat, along with the gun. Don't worry, after a few hours floating aimlessly in the sun, Patch will be dying of thirst, and if he drinks the seawater it will send him insane. He's truly doomed. It's the last you'll ever see of Patch.' Isaac locked the door and left.

Mollified by the thought of Patch going mad, Denim resigned himself to his own fate. Much later, two marines unlocked his shackles and marched him at gunpoint up to the main deck. The fresh air was stimulating, the sun blinding. Rubbing his eyes, he saw almost everyone on board ship was waiting to witness his trial. Pushed through the crowds, and up a small flight of steps to the quarterdeck, he faced his jury: Captain Bain, Lieutenant Thorpe, and two officers, all sat at a long trestle table. On the poop deck above, six armed marines and a drummer stood to attention.

So this was the man who had killed Blackie, thought Captain Bain, as he eyed Denim from head to toe. Now, with no one to inform him of traitors, the command of the ship would be forever in jeopardy. This young upstart needs to be taught a lesson. Banging the gavel hard on the table he started the proceedings.

From a scrolled parchment the first officer read aloud: 'Denim Armstrong, you are hereby charged with committing murder on Her Royal Majesty Queen Victoria's naval ship, the *Endurance*. The deceased, known only as Blackie, was stabbed and killed by your hand, and witnessed alike by officers and members of the crew. How plead you to these charges?'

Over the years, Denim had watched men beg for their lives at these mock trials, and always in vain. Unable to think of anything that would absolve him from blame, and knowing the verdict would be as the captain wished, he remained silent.

'Have you nothing to say in your defence?' asked Captain Bain. He was used to men pleading their innocence, but this young man was different. 'Take note, the prisoner has refused to answer.'

'Aye,' said the second officer, as he scribbled the account in the ship's ledger.

Staring coldly at Denim, Captain Bain picked up the gavel. He was about to decree judgement, when Lieutenant Thorpe leaned over and whispered. After some quiet deliberations between the two men, the captain cleared his throat, ready to speak. Wondering what high-seas justice was about to be bestowed on one of their shipmates, the crew pressed closer.

'It has been brought to my attention,' said the captain, 'that your work record is exemplary. But more important is the fact that you saved the life of Lieutenant Thorpe. And it is on these grounds that I have been asked to spare your life.'

Relief flooded Denim's brain like a drug. Was this a reprieve?

'However,' said the captain, 'the murder of one's shipmate cannot be condoned.'

The words made Denim hold his breath.

'Therefore, after careful thought, I have reconsidered my first impulse of having you strung up by the neck, and –' Pausing for a moment, he looked at the wide-eyed, grimy faces of the crew staring up at him through quarterdeck railings. Then, sombre faced, he turned to Denim. 'You will be keelhauled, no less than thrice!'

Gasps of shock arose from the crew. Lieutenant Thorpe looked in disbelief. He had tried to save Denim's life, but this archaic punishment, abolished by law, would kill him. Stoically, Denim showed no signs of emotion. But he remembered the strapping rogue of a man who was dragged under the hull of the ship three times. When pulled out of the sea, both arms had been severed. Word was, no one had ever survived three keelhauls.

'If you survive the keelhauling,' said Captain Bain as he glared at Denim, 'then you will spend the rest of your days on board this ship.' The gavel rattled the table. Punishment was to be immediate, ordered the Captain, as he retired to his cabin.

Steered windward, the ship slowed to a stop. Rope was threaded through a pulley on the starboard yardarm and taken under the belly of the ship by a diver to port side. Pulled through a second pulley on the opposite end of the yardarm, the rope spooled to the deck.

Stripped naked, Denim was trussed to the rope so he could not swim. A team of ten men hoisted him high into the air, on starboard side, until he was hanging over the sea. Slack rope was then pulled tight under the belly of the ship by the port side team. The man o' war was turned to the wind. When it was travelling at several knots, the teams lowered Denim to the sea, in time to the slow beat of the drum.

Filling his lungs to capacity, he sank into the cold, silent world. Each jerk of the rope pulled him deep towards the keel. Razor-sharp barnacles lodged on the hull cut into his flesh. Blood coloured the waters. Salt stung his wounds. Snatched under the belly of the ship, he propelled upwards towards port side. Feet first, he was hauled out of the sea. Gasping for air he yelled his pain.

'Take him back!' bellowed the first officer.

Strong currents slammed Denim hard against the ship. Winded, he struggled to hold onto his breath. As he reached the keel, he braced himself for the sharp tug of the rope that dragged him under, and upwards towards clear waters. Breaking the surface, he wheezed in the life-giving air.

'One keelhaul done,' shouted the officer.

Dropped back into the sea, Denim's head hit the hull. A large gash opened. Bubbles of air escaped his mouth. He gritted his teeth, and sank deeper. Scraped under the rib of the ship by a vigorous pull, he shot upwards. Coughing and choking, he was hoisted up on the port side.

A sudden squall hit the ship. Men fell about. The teams lost control of the rope. Denim splashed into the sea. Rogue currents sucked him deep below the keel. Recovering their positions the teams strained on the rope to pull Denim up. Half drowned, he was hoisted out of the ocean. Within seconds, the officer shouted and Denim was back in the depths. The journey took longer. His body was numb. He was losing all sense of time. Then he was above the waves, pulling in air, and then he was back in the sea.

Men crowded the starboard side, waiting to see if Denim could survive the last keelhaul. Some of them wanted to help pull him out, but they were afraid of being shot by the marines. The captain's rules were very strict.

'There he is!' screamed the sailors who had climbed the rigging for first sighting.

'Three keelhauls done,' shouted the first officer.

As the drumbeat stopped and the lifeless body was raised up to the yardarm, Captain Bain strolled across the quarterdeck. He wanted a closer look at the body hanging on the rope, but before he reached the railings, a deafening cheer erupted.

'He's alive,' shouted the men. 'He's alive!'

Denim's chest rose hard and fast. His head moved from side to side. Water spurted out of his mouth. His eyes opened.

'Remarkable,' mumbled Captain Bain. 'Most remarkable.' But when he heard the crew singing praises for their new hero, his admiration turned to scorn and a hostile dislike stoked deep inside. 'So the scurvy dogs think he's survived my judgement, do they? Lieutenant! Take him back into the water.'

'But captain, that's three keelhauls done.'

The captain's leathery face turned scarlet in anger. 'Take him back into the waters, I said!'

Knowing when not to disobey, Lieutenant Thorpe signalled the drummer, and the teams lowered Denim to the sea. Roars of protests hit the air. Some of the crew grabbed the rope to stop Denim's descent.

'Beat to quarters!' hollered Captain Bain to the drummer. *War Alert* pounded.

Within minutes, every marine on board ship was lined up in front of the quarterdeck. Bayonets fixed, they faced the rioters. Marines on the poop deck fired warning shots into the air. The rebels let go of the rope and Denim slid back into the depths.

Men ran to the other side of the ship and waited for Denim to be pulled out of the sea. But before they had a chance to see if he was still alive, he was submerged again. Loud objections from the crew were short lived as they moved over to starboard to await Denim's fate.

Captain Bain was bewildered. In all his years at sea, he had never heard of anyone surviving three keelhauls. Yes, Denim was young and strong, but many men had met that criteria. Vicious men, hardened by imprisonment in castle dungeons. Courageous men who had fought in battles and lived through terrible wars. Strong men, who had endured a much more arduous sea life than Denim. And yet they had not lived through this severe punishment. Why had he? If the man was allowed to live now, thought Captain Bain, he would become a living martyr, and the men would join him in future reprisals.

'Stop the drumbeat,' said Captain Bain to the lieutenant.

'What?' Lieutenant Thorpe shrieked.

'Stop the drumbeat, now. That's an order.'

'But captain, you cannot do that.'

'Damn it, man!' raged the captain. 'If you don't follow orders, I'll have *you* strung up on the nearest yardarm.'

Reluctantly, Lieutenant Thorpe gave the signal. The drumbeat ceased and the teams came to a standstill.

Denim had just reached the keel of the ship when he stopped moving through the water. What had happened? Had the rope snagged on something? Lungs burning for fresh air, he began to panic. Sharp needles of pain in his legs made him look down. A shoal of cleaner fish were feeding on his wounds. Then his heart almost stopped. Through the murky waters he saw a huge grey shark circling.

When the men realized that Denim wasn't being pulled out of the sea, they went wild with anger. Brandishing knives and cut-throats, they attacked the marines. The bosun tried to stop the uprising, but he was soon cut down. Musket fire from the marines felled scores of rebels as they broke through the thin red line. Officers fired randomly at gangs storming the quarterdeck. Two rebels were shot by Lieutenant Thorpe. Gunfire from the poop deck killed a handful more.

'We can't hold them, captain!' Lieutenant Thorpe became frantic. 'We've got to pull Denim out now, or we will all be killed!'

A bellicose roar filled the air as officers were overwhelmed by the rebels.

'Start the drum!' bellowed the captain. 'Start the drum!'

'Pull Denim out!' yelled the lieutenant. 'Pull Denim out!'

The rebels broke off their attack. Some ran to help the teams pull on the rope. The ship turned broadside to the wind and slowed to a stop.

The large grey shark homed in fast on Denim. He could see its small beady eyes and the saw-like teeth as its jaws opened wide. In those last few seconds of inevitable death, a terrific force snatched him under the keel. Faster than ever before, he was shooting upwards. Head throbbing with pain, his lungs screamed for air. He saw the clear water. Just a few seconds more. He had got to hang on. As bubbles of air jettisoned from his mouth, the water gushed in. Darkness engulfed him.

'There he is! There he is!' shouted the men who had climbed the rigging.

Denim's naked body was hoisted high. Blood trickled from a plethora of cuts. Head drooping, his long wet hair covered his face. There were no shouts of joy from the crew this time. Not a murmur could be heard as the forlorn figure swung gently in the breeze.

From the quarterdeck, Captain Bain scrutinized the body. There was no sign of life. Not even a twitch. With an all-knowing smirk, he turned to the lieutenant. 'So, he's just a mere mortal after all.'

Eyes moist, Lieutenant Thorpe stared at the pitiful sight hanging on the rope. This was the man who had saved his life, and yet he had been unable to save his.

A triumphant grin crossed the captain's face as he scoffed at the lieutenant's emotion. 'I guess he couldn't quite manage the fourth keelhaul.' Then, as if bored with the whole incident, he snapped, 'It's over! Leave the body hanging for a few days – it'll give this scurvy lot something to think about. Now lieutenant, get this rabble back to work, and let's get the ship moving.' Satisfied that his justice had been served, he disappeared inside the cabin.

With a great sense of loss, the crew moved quietly back to their work posts. One small group, hesitant to leave, stared doggedly at the body hanging on the rope. Moments ago, they had all shouted Denim's praises, and now he was dead.

'Look, he moved,' someone whispered. The rest of the group stared hard. Then whispers turned into shouts. Men who had moved away came running back to see if it was true.

'Yes, he moved again!'

'I saw him,' said another.

Denim's body trembled. His legs began to shake. 'It's the devil's jig,' shouted the superstitious, and edged away. White foam erupted from Denim's mouth as he choked up gurgles of seawater.

'He's alive! He's alive,' shouted the group. Hearing the jubilant cries, Captain Bain came onto the quarterdeck to investigate. When he saw Denim glaring at him, he gasped in astonishment.

'We have got to let him live, captain,' pleaded Lieutenant Thorpe. 'The whole crew are behind him now.'

Captain Bain turned to face five hundred and more men who were bawling mercy for Denim, and he knew that ninety marines armed with muskets, and only twelve officers with pistols, would not be enough to quell an uprising. Yes, dozens of the scourge would be shot before they overwhelmed the ranks, but it would mean certain death for him and the officers. 'Very well, set him free,' growled the captain.

With joy in his heart, Lieutenant Thorpe shouted to the men, 'Set Denim free!' Cries of approval came from all quarters as Denim was lowered onto a stretcher and taken to sick bay. Dead bodies were disposed of, and the crew were slowly cajoled back to their duties.

Irate that command of the ship had been compromised by the young upstart, Captain Bain slammed the cabin door. Somehow, he had to get rid of him. Tomorrow, they would dock in Port Royal, Jamaica, before sailing north to Virginia to escort an ambassador back to England; but he had no intention of letting Denim live long enough to see the Americas.

Chapter 7

The Storm

Captain Bain knew that many of the marines and officers were friendly with Denim and that if anything untoward should happen to him – especially now that he held the status of a hero – there would be an instant revolt. For his plan to work, he needed someone who was unscrupulous and held loyalties to no one.

Summoned to the captain's quarters, Razvan was a worried man until a neat tot of brandy was pushed across the table. Knocking the drink back, he eyed the captain and wondered what game was afoot.

'Within the hour, we will be docking in Port Royal,' said Captain Bain, 'and while some of the crew and officers are taking shore leave, I want you to pay a little visit to sick bay.' He threw a small bag of Spanish doubloons on the table and looked at the gypsy's shifty eyes to see if he was grasping the implication. 'And it would be of no surprise to me, or anyone else, if Denim didn't recover from the ordeal of being keelhauled. Do you understand?'

Gold coins made Razvan's eyes light up. Thoughts of killing Denim so excited him that slaver drooled through his black teeth and down his stubbly chin. He wiped his face with the cuff of his dirty sleeve and cautiously picked up the bounty. 'Aye aye, captain. I gets your meaning, but...' Eyebrows raised, he looked at the captain. 'But what if anyone should spot anything, er... untoward, like?'

Liaising with such low life was against the captain's principles, but on this occasion it was necessary. 'Officers left on board ship will be handpicked by me and they will turn a blind eye to your activities,' said Captain Bain. 'When I come back from shore leave, I shall expect good news. Do you follow?'

'To be sure, captain, to be sure.'

'If you say a word to anyone about this meeting, then it will be *you* who faces the gallows. Do you understand?'

'Aye aye, captain. Aye aye.'

'Very well. Dismissed!'

Once moored in Port Royal, gangplanks were lowered onto the *Endurance* and trusted crewmen and officers went ashore. Following the captain into the busy town, Lieutenant Thorpe was assigned the job of negotiating fresh supplies from the markets.

After watching the exodus from the ship, Razvan paid two of his cronies to make Denim's death look natural. Then he diverted the surgeon away from sick bay. While Denim slept, the two men tiptoed to the bedside and pulled the straw pillow over his face. Unable to fend off the attack, Denim had almost breathed his last when the pillow was suddenly snatched away. One assailant, throat cut, fell dead across the bed. The other put up a strong fight, until a sword thrust to the belly dropped him to the floor. Blade dripping blood, the victor came towards Denim.

'Lieutenant Thorpe!' exclaimed Denim in surprise. 'Thank God it is you.'

'Looks like I got here just in time. When the captain gave me the quartermaster's job of buying fresh supplies, I thought something was amiss. So I arranged delivery of the goods and rushed back to the ship.'

'Lieutenant Thorpe, I am forever in your debt.'

'You were lucky this time Denim, but I would sleep lightly if I were you. I feel sure the captain was behind this attempt on your life, and he may well try again. I'll send someone down to remove the bodies – meanwhile you make haste and get well.'

Sitting in the cosy snug room of the Jolly Roger tavern, Captain Bain was confident that the treachery on board ship was being committed right now. While eating thin slices of pure white coconut, washed down with sips of Jamaican rum, he was surprised when two well-dressed gentlemen approached and introduced themselves.

It soon became evident, when they asked him to deliver a cargo of arms to North Virginia, that they were dissidents of the Southern slave trade. Knowing it was illegal to transport such goods, Captain Bain refused. But when four velvet bags of gold doubloons were offered, and a bonus was suggested for delivering on a certain date, he shook hands on the deal. Placing the four bags inside his long blue tunic, he left the tavern.

At the quayside, he could see that Lieutenant Thorpe had been over-zealous in the purchase of food supplies. If all the crates were taken on board, there would not be enough room to hide the illegal cargo. Reasoning that they would easily make it to Virginia, he gave orders to leave half of the goods behind.

Captain Bain made haste to the cabin. He locked the door behind him and pulled the old sea chest out from underneath the bed. Pushing aside letters, keepsakes, and a large dagger, he hid the four velvet bags of gold inside. A loud knock on the cabin door startled him. He closed the sea chest, and shoved it under the bed. Then he unlocked the door.

Lieutenant Thorpe entered and reported the attack on Denim.

'Have the offenders been caught?' Captain Bain asked.

'Two would-be killers are dead, but Denim's alive and well.' Lieutenant Thorpe enjoyed breaking that part of the news.

So the stupid gypsy had failed, thought Captain Bain. Without showing his anger he informed the lieutenant that an extra cargo was being delivered at midnight, and to have able bodies ready to load it on board ship.

When the belfry bell clanged midnight, three horse-drawn wagons rolled down the deserted quay and came alongside the ship. Harbour guards, bribed by Captain Bain, kept out of sight as the crates of contraband were smuggled on board. At first light, the *Endurance* set sail.

Over the following days, Denim made a full recovery. The crew hailed him as some kind of demi-god; the only man known to have survived four keelhauls. His survival bolstered their courage and, without a bosun to keep them in check, they dared to take liberties.

Denim's popularity was a constant source of worry for Captain Bain, for he was sure that the men would unite at some point and take over the ship. With three weeks left before they reached the Americas, he had to think of a way to deflate the men's support for Denim.

Wondering why he had been summoned to the captain's cabin, Denim was surprised how spacious the living quarters were. Sunshine streamed through the skylight, highlighting a silver candelabrum placed in the centre of a long, mahogany dining table surrounded by eight chairs. Two wall lamps in a partitioned alcove gave view to a small library of maritime books. In the furthest corner, a blanket overhung the bunk bed and partly hid the old sea chest underneath. At a large desk littered with maps, a sextant, compass, and telescope, Captain Bain and Lieutenant Thorpe sat facing him.

A standing officer read aloud from a scrolled document: 'Denim Armstrong, you are hereby appointed bosun, on the good ship *Endurance*. Your duties are as follows: chargehand of all sailors on board ship, with exception of the marines; you will pledge allegiance to your captain and his fellow officers, and enforce their orders at all times without question.'

'For this upgrade of duty, you will receive an increase of wages, extra rations of food, and an additional gallon of grog per day. Freedom of the ship is yours, but the quarterdeck and the poop deck will be out of bounds. Previous convictions stand: to serve in the Queen's Royal Navy for the rest of your natural life.'

Placing the document on the table, the officer offered Denim a quill dipped in ink and asked him to sign. Denim saw through the captain's ploy. In the last ten years, the ship had lost as many bosuns and he knew that if he were to fill the position, the very same men who worshipped him now would turn against him. Chances of living long as a bosun were slim, but freedom of the ship was paramount in his quest for revenge – so he signed.

Following Denim outside the cabin, Lieutenant Thorpe offered his assistance. 'I'll try to help you where I can, Denim, but please remember I too have orders to follow.' Knowing the lieutenant was sincere, Denim thanked him.

'Oh, and there's something else,' said the lieutenant. He unbuttoned the top pocket on his tunic jacket and took out the gold locket and chain. 'I understand this belonged to Pegs. I believe you should have it.'

Placing the locket around his neck, Denim vowed to keep it forever, in memory of Pegs.

It did not take long for Denim to acquire the traits needed for his new role, and he exercised his authority in the strictest of manners. Managing all disputes that arose between the men, he made sure they adhered to the captain's demands and kept them hard at work.

Opposition to him escalated, and his life was threatened on more than one occasion. He suspected Razvan and his gang of cut-throats as the main conspirators, for he knew they would stop at nothing to get even for the death of their leader. There was no honour among the lowlife on board this ship: kill or be killed was the rule. Boxing lessons, and the knife fighting that Pegs had taught him, were his saviour, as he learned to kill any crew member who opposed him.

Captain Bain turned a blind eye to crewmen disappearing at sea. In reality, he knew what was taking place, but providing Denim's vicious tactics were discreet, and kept the men in line, all was well. Replacements could soon be reaped from the drunken orgies in the beer taverns at any port.

Several days of excellent weather saw the *Endurance* on schedule, but an outbreak of scurvy and news from the chief purser that some food stocks had turned rotten, and that water barrels had gone green, made Captain Bain ponder. Had he erred, by leaving fresh supplies on the harbour of Port Royal?

'Land ahoy!' was shouted from the crow's nest. Captain Bain considered the options: if they explored the island for fresh fruit and water, at least one day's sailing would be lost; the illegal cargo would be delivered late; and he would lose the bonus payment. Also, while moored, Denim might find an opportunity to seize the ship. With only seven days left to their destination, he took a chance on the good weather prevailing and the scurvy being contained. The helmsman was ordered to sail on by.

For three days, strong winds kept the ship on schedule and, with only a dozen new cases of scurvy reported, Captain Bain was satisfied that he had made the right decision. A few days more would see them in Virginia. With high expectations of collecting the bonus, he made plans to have Denim hanged for treason the moment they landed in port.

That evening, he invited six officers to his cabin to celebrate the success of the voyage. Skylight shutters were closed to give privacy from the poop deck, and the silver candelabrum was lit. Food fit for a king was laid out on the long dining table by the galley cook and his mate. Two small casks were opened, and the best of the ship's wine was served in drinking glasses.

Heading the table, Captain Bain listened to the officers sitting either side of him exchange pleasantries about their lives and past voyages. When the evening feast was over, and the drinks were flowing freely, Captain Bain commandeered the officers' small talk with his rhetoric of historic sea battles. Halfway through his favourite telling of

'Trafalgar', a constant battering on the skylight made them all look up.

'Hailstone?' queried the first officer.

'Damn it,' Captain Bain cursed. 'A storm! That's the last thing I need.'

Moving outside, the party observed the overcast sky. 'It's going to be a bad one, I fear,' said the second officer.

'Alert the crew,' grumbled Captain Bain.

As the officers dashed to rouse the crew, the sea became choppy and the hailstones turned into a deluge of rain.

'All hands on deck!'

'All hands on deck!'

Warning bells clanged. Sleeping crewmen fell out of their hammocks and scrambled aloft. Within minutes, the ship was manned for battle stations. Orders were shouted from every corner as the gale-force winds mauled the ship.

'Secure all hatches!'

'Batten down!'

'Close the gun ports!'

'Furl the sails!'

Like monkeys climbing palm trees, men clambered up the rigging and hauled in the huge canvas sails. Squads of men raced along the decks to fasten down the boats. Cannons were pulled back and portholes closed. Objects that were not fixed were tied down.

Deafening thunderclaps vibrated across the ocean. Jagged streaks of white lightning ripped open the dark sky. A huge fireball trailed across the heavens and plummeted into the sea. Enormous waves rocked the ship. Scores of men were washed overboard. Splinters of flame showered the deck as a thunderbolt exploded into the topgallant mast. Crashing below, the mast pinned several men to the deck.

Officers and marines lay down their guns, and worked alongside the crew. Armies of men carrying buckets of tar ran to bung the leaks in the hold, while gangs were sent to the pumphouse and the bilge to bail out water. The helmsman's team was thrown to the floor as hurricane winds dictated direction and the steering wheel spun wildly. Like a child's toy lost in the froth, the ship went into a spin. Forced high by giant swells and then low into deep troughs, men toppled from the rigging. Gunners were crushed under cannons that broke loose from straining ropes. A cutter ripped away from its davit and crashed into the sea. Pounding waves smashed it against the bow. Men dropped from sheer exhaustion as they battled throughout the night to keep the ship afloat.

As the flooding seawater buffeted lifeless bodies this way and that across the deck, Captain Bain lay on his bed and prayed that the ship would not sink.

Chapter 8

Mutiny

Golden beams of sunshine played upon the captain's face. He opened his eyes and stared at the skylight. He had listened to the howling winds of the storm all night until falling asleep, but now there was an unusual silence. Rising from the bed, he put the tricorn hat on his head and went outside the cabin to investigate.

Under a gentle breeze, the ship was drifting aimlessly over calm seas. Masses of foamy brine clung to the decks and the rigging. Chains, cables and ropes trailed from broken yardarms. Torn sails hung down as in the aftermath of a war battle. Bodies lay everywhere. He could hear feeble groans of men trapped under the gallant mast. Spotting a warrant officer coming out of the hatch, he beckoned him over and asked for a report on the damage.

'Most of the leaks have been bunged,' said the warrant officer, 'but the hold was flooded and some food supplies have been contaminated. One of the cutters was lost out at sea.'

'Find the chief purser,' said the captain, 'tell him to salvage what food he can. And I want guards on the ammunitions and water supplies.'

As the warrant officer left, Lieutenant Thorpe and the first officer appeared.

'How many men have we lost?' asked Captain Bain.

'Two officers are missing and at least forty men are dead,' said the first officer.

'Find the sailmaker,' said Captain Bain. 'All

damaged sails must be replaced immediately. And get a team of carpenters working on the gallant mast. I want everything ship-shape within two hours.'

'Aye aye, captain,' said the first officer as he left to follow orders.

'Has the ship's surgeon survived the storm?' asked Captain Bain.

'Yes,' said Lieutenant Thorpe. 'He's tending the injured, right now.'

'How many men are in sick bay?'

'Three score are laid up with scurvy, but dozens more are suffering from fatigue.'

'Humph!' scoffed the captain. 'Any man that says he's too ill to work, have him thrown overboard. We'll soon find out who the shirkers are.' Captain Bain looked at the groaning bodies lying about the decks. 'Any man here gets to his feet, give him a tot of rum. Then get these bilge rats back to work. I want this ship seaworthy as soon as possible.'

Lieutenant Thorpe went to rally the workforce, and two midshipmen came running to the captain's call. After studying the maps, on the table, inside the cabin, they discovered that the ship had been blown off course by two days. As they plotted a new course for Virginia, the helmsman came to report that the ship was stuck in the 'doldrums'.

'Damn it!' Captain Bain cursed. 'Is everything against me?' He banged his fist down hard on the table as he thought about losing the bonus payment. 'Lower the pinnace. We'll tow this damned ship to Virginia if needs be. I intend getting back on schedule, even if it means working this mangy crew day and night. And by Jove, if any man slacks his duties, I'll have him flogged to death.' Silence filled the room. 'Well, what are you waiting for?' ranted the captain. All three officers excused themselves and left.

Ropes put around the capstan, were fastened to the pinnace as it was lowered to the sea. At the helmsman's command sixteen men slaved at the oars and the mighty man o' war was tugged across the millpond waters. Before midday, they had rowed into fresh winds. The giant sails ballooned and, as the ship picked up speed, the pinnace was winched back on board.

Trying to make up for lost time, Captain Bain worked the crew even harder. Instead of coasting safely at night, the ship was now driven through dangerous dark waters, and slackers were beaten readily with the captain's cane. With only meagre rations of food, the crew's morale began to decline.

This ill fortune was the chance Denim had been waiting for. Secretly, he gathered the hardiest members of the crew, and put forward a daring plan of mutiny. 'When the master of arms and his corporals have completed the midnight patrol, only a handful of marines will be left on duty; while the officers are sleeping, this will be the best chance to take over the ship... What say you, men?' The 'ayes' were unanimous. They all knew that if anyone could lead them to victory, it was Denim.

It was almost midnight when the mutineers congregated on the lower gun deck. Armed with cutthroats and anything else they could use as weapons, they crept stealthily towards the aft where the junior officers were housed. The inexperienced officers were soon contained and put under guard.

As the mutineers sneaked towards the middle gun deck, more men joined them. Without a single shot being fired, the sleeping marines were quickly captured. Those that resisted were clubbed unconscious. Denim split the gang into two groups and, while he led a dozen men to the poop deck, the second group charged through the wooden partitions of the wardroom. As they surrounded the senior officials, two officers made a grab for their pistols. They were quickly shot, and the rest gave in without a fight.

Alerted by the gunshots, the duty marines on the poop deck saw Denim and his gang lurking in the shadows and opened fire. Within minutes, six marines lay dead at the expense of nine mutineers. Poop deck secured, Denim made haste to the captain's cabin. Barging through the door, a single shot missed him by inches, killing the mutineer behind. He grabbed the pistol off the captain and pushed him into the hands of the rebels that had followed. 'Throw him in the brig, men, but make sure no harm comes to him or the officers – we may have need of them later.'

Denim reloaded the pistol and slipped it into his waistband. He dragged the dead mutineer out of the door and locked himself inside the cabin. Opening the old sea chest, he shoved letters and keepsakes aside and picked up the large dagger. He noticed the piece of flint, welded into the end of the white bone handle. Then he saw the four velvet bags. Each held a small fortune in gold doubloons. Placing everything back inside the chest, he shoved it under the bed.

Relaxing on the bunk bed, he stared at the stars through the skylight. He could hear the mutineers celebrating their victory as they fired random shots into the air. No doubt they had raided the ammunition stocks and the liquor stores. He knew there would be no stopping their rampage tonight.

As he made plans for tomorrow, he absentmindedly twirled the chain around his neck and the gold locket fell to the floor. On impact, it sprang open and revealed a portrait. Etched inside was a name: Katie Adams. Replacing the locket around his neck, he wondered why Pegs had never spoken of her. Curious to know more, he went to Pegs' secret hiding place.

The sleeping quarters were deserted. In the dark room, moonbeams shining through a porthole showed the way. He knelt below the hammock where Pegs had once slept, and removed a loose floorboard. Pulling out a small trinket box, he found it empty. Careful inspection revealed a false inset with a folded letter. He held the message up to the moonlight and read it.

To my dear friend,

If you are reading this letter, then I am no longer alive and you have found my fondest keepsake. Inside the gold locket is a picture of Katie, the only true love that I have ever known. During my early years at sea, the Endurance *anchored at a port named Boston Wharf. While waiting for a late cargo to arrive, shore leave was granted, and I visited Rosie's Cantina. There, I met and fell in love with one of the dancing girls, Katie Adams.*

To show her devotion, she gave me this locket and pledged that she would wait for me, no matter how long. I promised Katie that I would find a way back to her. But alas, the ship never returned to Boston Wharf. Tormented by love, I tried to escape the ship, but I was caught and punished. After that, it became impossible to gain my freedom. During my years of heartache, I have always wondered if Katie waited for me, or if she married another.

If you should ever be in the south of the Americas and you happen to come across Boston Wharf, my dying wish would be for you to visit Rosie's Cantina and seek out Katie. Give her the locket and explain why I never returned – but, most of all, let her know of my undying love.

I am ever your friend, Pegs

P.S.

During our years together on board the Endurance*, I have loved you as a father would a son. And I know that one day you will achieve what I was never able to do: escape the ship. I wish I could be with you, Denim, but my life is done. Good luck to you, my dearest of friends.*

Denim's eyes filled with sadness. Folding the letter back inside the trinket box, he hid it under the boards. Sitting on his haunches, he thought how fitting it was for the letter to sail the seas forever, in memory of Pegs.

Bang! The explosion made him jump. A ball of lead whistled by his head. He dived under the hammock for safety. Hardly daring to breathe, he waited. A shadowy figure crept closer. Denim kicked out. The man crashed to the floor. His pistol exploded again as it hit the boards and slid out of reach. Diving on top of him, Denim seized the man by the throat. Like an animal trapped in a snare, his legs kicked wildly. A repugnant smell stung Denim's nostrils. He tightened his grip. Only when the body beneath him became still, did he jump to his feet.

Moonbeams played upon black teeth protruding from the man's gaping jaws. Denim's revenge list was shortening: first Blackie and now Razvan. Only Captain Bain remained.

Chapter 9

Revenge is Sweet

Feeling safer than he had for years, Denim had slept soundly. He unlocked the cabin door, and in glorious sunshine, he strolled onto the quarterdeck. The ship was sailing without direction. On the decks below he could see drunken men lying everywhere. It was time to take command, he decided. Pacing the main deck, he saw two rebels awakening from their indulgences, and told them to fetch Captain Bain from the cells below.

Denim clanged the belfry bell, and then jumped onto a large wooden crate. 'Come on you drunken layabouts, wake up! Wake up, I say!'

Hardly a body moved.

'Wake up you scoundrels, wake up!' Men rolled over and groaned, but when they saw the captain being brought to the fore, they wondered what all the fuss was about and staggered to their feet.

'Come on you drunken rogues,' shouted Denim. 'Tell me, what are we to do with this beloved captain of ours?'

One man, still swigging grog, shouted back, 'Make him walk the plank!' The remark caused a few grunts, but the idea soon caught on.

'String the old sea dog up!'

'Aye, let the birds strip him clean!'

'Run the mangy devil through with a cutlass!'

'This is treason, you fools,' shouted the captain. 'You will all end up on the gallows for this treachery.' Mocking laughter drowned him out.

'String him up now!' growled one of the men.

'Keelhaul him!' spat another.

Denim grabbed the captain's tricorn hat and placed it on his own head, much to the delight of the drunken rogues that watched. Feeling foolish, Captain Bain pleaded, 'Listen to me, men. I can help you. I can help you all...' His words became inaudible as the rebels blasphemed and cursed. In despair, he turned to Denim. 'Give command of the ship back to me, and I will release you at the next port. You can have your freedom and I will recommend a pardon for all your crimes.'

The rebels suddenly became louder and more aggressive. They started to close in.

Shaking in fear, Captain Bain turned to Denim as his only hope. 'I have gold. You can have it all, as well as your freedom.' At the mention of gold, the bloodthirsty rebels hushed to hear what Denim would say.

'Ah!' exclaimed Denim, feigning a look of surprise. 'Gold you say?'

'Yes,' said Captain Bain, 'I have three bags of gold. You can have it all.'

Denim laughed at the captain's lie. 'But I have already found the gold, and there are four bags not three.' The captain's blubbering excuses were drowned out by the rebels' loud hoorays; there was more gold to be had.

Holding his hands high, Denim quietened the men and then pointed his finger at the captain. 'Now let me think... I have got your gold and I have got your ship, and... I've got you!' Guffaws of laughter, from the rebels, filled the air.

'Men! Enough of this tomfoolery,' shouted Denim, tiring of the charade. 'Bring out the rope.' Several mutineers came running with a coil and quickly made a noose.

Captain Bain's legs almost gave way. 'Don't hang me, Denim. Please don't hang me.'

From the large crate that he was standing on, Denim stuck his boot on the captain's chest, and kicked him backwards into the arms of the rebels. 'No, my dear captain, hanging is too good for you. Perhaps a bit of keelhauling would be more to your liking!'

Captain Bain screamed in terror. 'No! No! I'm too old, Denim. I'm too old.'

His laments fell on deaf ears. Denim knew the men's anger was high and they wanted revenge. If he was to show any compassion now, the men would turn on him too.

'Please, don't keelhaul me, Denim, I beg of you. Show mercy, please show some mercy.'

'As you wish,' said Denim, jumping down from the crate. 'We won't keelhaul you.'

Weeping with relief, the captain crawled on his knees and fawned at Denim's feet. 'Oh, thank you Denim, thank you. You will be rewarded many times, many times.' A loud roar of protest arose from the rebels.

Denim pulled the pistol from his waistband and fired it into the air. 'Listen men, we haven't got time to keelhaul him. Instead, we're going to drag him from the aft.' Raptures of delight came from the rebels as they closed in on the captain.

'No! No!' shrieked the captain. 'Don't let them do it, Denim,'

'Take him to the stern, men,' shouted Denim, 'and throw him over.'

With the noose tied around the captain's wrists, the rebels dragged him across the deck. At the taffrail, they picked him up above their heads. 'The sharks are going to have you for breakfast,' they shouted.

'No! No!' shrieked Captain Bain. 'You can't do this. I'm the captain, I'm the captain...' His screams could still be heard as he hit the ocean waves.

'Man the ship, men,' yelled Denim. He threw the captain's hat high into the air. 'We're on our way to freedom.' A unanimous roar of joy sounded from the rebels as they ran to their stations.

'Drop the sails, men, and let's reap the wind,' Denim shouted. Within minutes the rigging came alive. The helmsman's wheel turned and the ship lurched forward. With a full spread of canvas showing, the mighty man o' war ploughed through the waters, dragging Captain Bain in its wake.

Chapter 10

New Country New Dangers

The death of Captain Bain brought a new impetus to the mutineers as they worked vigorously and in harmony. But after three days of meagre rations of food and water, they became despondent. Scurvy was rampant and bodies were disposed of daily. If they did not reach land soon, thought Denim, they were all doomed.

Escorted from the cells below, Lieutenant Thorpe entered the cabin. Although Denim greeted him informally, the lieutenant remained silent. Clearly, the mutiny had put them against one another, but when Denim explained the grave situation, the lieutenant relented.

'When we reach land what are your intentions?' asked Lieutenant Thorpe.

'The mutineers will abandon the ship and leave command to you.'

'If I help you now, how do I know I will not be killed as soon as land is sighted?'

'I guarantee your safety,' said Denim, 'and the lives of your fellow officers. You have my solemn oath on that.' He offered out his hand to seal the pact.

Lieutenant Thorpe knew there was every chance that the mutineers might kill him and the officers before escaping; for many a grudge had been born over the years against the hierarchy that governed the ship. But accepting Denim's oath now might be the best chance of survival. He had always admired Denim for his courage, and believed him trustworthy. After all, this was the man who had saved his life. He grabbed the hand offered and shook his agreement.

'On your word of honour?'

'You have it,' declared Denim.

'Then I shall need a midshipman to plot a new course, and the helmsman to steer the ship.'

'As you wish,' said Denim. 'They will be brought up from the cells immediately, and you and your two officers can make this cabin your base.'

Three days' sailing brought the Virginian coastline into sight. While Lieutenant Thorpe and his two officers were engaged at the helm, Denim summoned the leaders of the mutiny to the cabin and told them his plan.

'Within two hours we will reach the port. If we sail in at night, we will be mistaken for an enemy ship and sunk by the harbour's defence artillery. Therefore, we will approach in daylight. Half a league out, we will drop anchor and display warning flags to say that there is malady on board. This will explain why the captain and his officers will not be coming ashore in the barge, as customary.' Listening intently, the men nodded their approval.

'At nightfall, all the men who can't swim will arm themselves with muskets and pistols from the ship's arsenal and take to the boats. The rest will take knives and swords and swim alongside, to the harbour. All in favour?' The 'ayes' were unanimous.

'Once ashore, it will be every man for himself,' said Denim, 'but at least there will be a chance of freedom. Any man that chooses to stay on board will face British justice, and likely the gallows. Is there anything else?'

'What about the gold?' demanded one surly voice.

Suspicious eyes glared at Denim, but he had already anticipated their question. He pulled three bags of gold doubloons out of the sea chest and threw them on the table. 'Share this among the men.'

Greedily, the leaders grabbed the money and left the cabin. Denim suspected that they would keep the gold for themselves, but he did not care. Tying the fourth bag of gold around his waist, along with the white bone-handled dagger, he picked up the captain's telescope and joined the rebels on the main deck.

When the bastions of the harbour came into sight, the best bower anchor was dropped. An officer learned in the art of arranging pennants was brought from the cells below and ordered to display a message stating that there was a sickness on board ship, and that they were staying in quarantine for a few days as a precaution.

Unable to read the pennants, and doubting that any of the other mutineers could, Denim pointed the pistol at the officer and warned him, 'If there is any indication that you have informed the harbour officials of the mutiny, then you'll be joining Davy Jones's locker at the bottom of the sea.'

The message was hoisted high up on the mast. Shortly, a line of pennants showed from one of the castle turrets in the harbour.

'What's their reply?' asked Denim, handing the telescope over to the officer.

'They acknowledge and await further instruction,' said the officer.

Denim retrieved the telescope and, when he was certain that no boats were setting sail to investigate, the officer was taken back to the cells. As he scanned the harbour for activity, he swept his viewpoint across the shoreline to a sandy inlet, between two craggy reefs. With a smile of satisfaction, he closed the telescope.

As night befell the harbour, Denim locked the lieutenant and the two officers in the cabin and went to organize the mutineers. A large group of men, hoping for a pardon, had decided to stay on board. To the most trusted of this group he handed a few weapons, but with a warning to protect Lieutenant Thorpe, for he was their best chance of getting a pardon.

Returning to the cabin, Denim made Lieutenant Thorpe aware of the situation. 'Some of the crew are staying on board ship. They have guns, but they're under orders to protect you until the harbour officials arrive.'

'I need a gun,' said Lieutenant Thorpe, assertively.

Denim knew that if he had met the lieutenant under different circumstances, they would have been the best of friends. He pulled the pistol out of his waistband and handed it over. 'Take this, it's already loaded.'

Lieutenant Thorpe smiled. 'Thanks, and good luck to you, Denim.'

'And to you too, lieutenant,' said Denim, as he locked the cabin door and went to join the mutineers.

The pinnace and the cutters were lowered to the sea. Two hundred men slid down ropes and scrambled onto the boats. Swimmers kicked off their shoes and, with knives gripped between their teeth, they followed Denim's lead into the sea. As the small armada paddled softly towards the harbour, heavy storm clouds blanked the moon. Without anyone noticing, Denim dropped to the rear of the invasion and swam to the sandy inlet between the two rocky crags.

It had always been his intention to desert the

renegades, for he knew his best chance of survival was to travel alone. Wading ashore, he checked the bag of gold and the dagger. Barefoot, he climbed the cliffs facing him. On reaching the summit, he lost his balance and slipped down the slopes on the other side. None the worse for his fall, he got to his feet and ran in the opposite direction of the harbour.

He had not gone far inland when he heard the roar of artillery and wailing cries. A thunderous explosion lit up the skyline. He stopped to look back as the harbour became ablaze. Some mutineers must have reached the gunpowder stores, he thought. As he distanced himself from the bedlam, he realized that the officer who had displayed the pennants must have warned the harbour authorities about the mutiny. The men would have walked into a trap; they wouldn't have stood a chance. With those sombre thoughts, he increased his pace.

Eventually, the battle sounds faded, and the night recovered its tranquillity. Occasionally, he was startled by the jack rabbits which bounded out of unseen hiding places, and which then scurried back into the darkness. At one time, an unearthly screech stopped him dead in his tracks. When silence prevailed, he ran on again, guessing that some nocturnal predator had just caught its prey. Suddenly, the threatening storm clouds gave up their load. Like a drowned rat with nowhere to shelter, he ran on through the night.

Early morning sun steam-dried his clothes. Feet bleeding, Denim slowed to a walking pace. He was beginning to wonder if there were any inhabitants in this part of the country, when a log cabin and two large outbuildings next to a small copse came into sight. The chimney stack was not smoking. The occupants must still be sleeping, he thought as he approached the quiet dwelling.

Cautiously, he entered the first outbuilding. A large fowl pen contained chickens. He cracked open a number of eggs and ate the raw contents, but when the hens started to make a fuss, he moved to the next building. Inside the stables he quenched his thirst from the water trough. Several horses had been bedded down for the night. He pulled a saddle off the wooden rail and strapped it on a black stallion.

As he pinned the stable doors open to lead the stallion out, dogs started barking from inside the cabin. Panicking, he jumped onto the horse, and galloped away from the buildings.

Gunshots boomed. 'Stop thief, stop!' a man shouted as he came running out of the cabin. Two red setters gave chase. Denim kicked the stallion into top speed and the dogs returned to their master. As he made his getaway, he could hear the owner kicking and cursing the dogs for letting an intruder escape.

Riding until sunset, Denim came to a valley where boulders had rolled down craggy hillsides and formed a rock pool. Tufts of wild maize had grown close to the water's edge, while dense thickets of gorse and spruce trees surrounded the area. At the receding end of the valley, fields of buffalo grass stretched all the way to timberlands in the far-off distance.

He quenched his thirst and tethered the horse to a lone cactus next to the pool, and then he collected deadwood from the undergrowth. Piling the sticks beside a tree, he rolled a handful of straw into a wiry ball, struck the flint embedded in the handle of the dagger with a small rock, and sparked a fire. He cut strips from his shirt and bandaged his bleeding feet.

Then, stabbing the dagger upright in the ground next to the bag of gold, he laid back against the tree to enjoy the warmth of the fire.

Chewing on a handful of maize, he gazed at the uncountable stars. What a beautiful night, he thought. He considered his plans. Armed only with a dagger, he knew he would not be able to kill any wild game, and starved of wholesome food, he needed to reach a town – and soon. A cold gust made him stoke the fire. Flames licked high into the night. Saddle sore and weary from a full day's riding, he fell asleep.

A few hours later, Denim awoke with a start. Wide eyed, he looked about him. All was quiet and still. The fire had burned low. Dark clouds trailing across the moon, cast foreboding shadows around the camp. A shooting star arced in the inky black night and faded. Leaves rustled in the trees, as a gust of wind made the fire cinders glow red. He threw on more sticks. Flames roared, and the visibility of the camp widened. A shudder of fear went down his spine. The horse was gone. Had something frightened it away?

Straining his eyes and ears, Denim searched for an intruder, but there was no sign of anything amiss. What had awakened him? He could feel goose-bumps as the hair on his nape rose. Then his heart sank. Two green eyes glowed out of the darkness. Fear stricken, he grabbed the dagger. The shiny blade flashed reflections of firelight into the thickets. Green eyes disappeared.

Denim tried to calm his fears. Perhaps a deer was foraging in the night, or some other harmless animal. Flames dwindled. The pile of sticks was low; he decided to collect more. As he stood up an unearthly howl shook the night air. He fell back against the tree. Scrambling on all fours, he threw the last of the sticks on the fire. Like Chinese fireworks, the flames crackled and spluttered high; but whatever had made that hideous sound was nowhere in sight. And yet he knew it was out there, watching him, and when the fire burned out it would attack.

After all the trials and tribulations Denim had suffered on the ship, is this how he was to end? To die here, alone, in the jaws of some ferocious carnivore? Now he wished he had kept the pistol that he had given to Lieutenant Thorpe. Dagger at the ready, and not daring to move, he waited.

As the fire burned low, dark perimeters of the camp crept closer. Denim heard something move in the bushes. He felt himself tremble. Green eyes had returned. Quickly, he grabbed the last burning stick from the fire and threw it hard. The fiery torch whirled through the air and landed in front of a huge timber wolf. Denim gasped at the sight. His hand tightened on the dagger. He knew wolves hunted in packs. This one was alone. Surely, it would not attack.

With low grumbling growls the wolf's hungry eyes fixed on Denim. The fiery torch suddenly flickered out and the wolf was gone. As the campfire burned to ash, darkness engulfed him. Then a silence, the like of which Denim had never known, made him press his back against the tree. He held his breath to listen, and stared into the gloomy blackness. Sweat beaded on his forehead. Nervous muscles tightened for action.

Bounding paws thudded towards him. A ghost-like apparition sprang out of the night. Knocked to the ground, the wolf was over of him. Snarling fangs snapped inches away as Denim held onto its furry neck. Saliva streamed onto his face. With his legs locked over the animal's back, man and beast entwined they rolled over the hot coals. Clouds of ash fumed the air.

Powerful jaws locked tight onto Denim's shoulder. Incisors bit deep. Hind claws ripped into his thighs. Again and again, he struck out with the dagger, until the blade lodged deep in the animal's flank. Losing hold of the knife, both hands squeezed hard on the wolf's neck. In a frenzy, the beast jumped, turned, and twisted. It tried to shake off the thing that was choking the life out of it.

Dragged this way and that across the rocky terrain, Denim clung on until the wolf came to a sudden standstill. Panting heavily, its jaws released its hold. Blood spewed from its mouth. Body quivering, it gave a soulful whimper and sagged on top of its killer. Unable to move, with wounds bleeding profusely, Denim blacked out.

Winds blowing down the valley made graceful waves in the fields of buffalo grass. As the night gave way to the morn, the moon's reflection in the rock pool faded. It would be another hour before full daylight, but already a gopher was busy at work extending its maze of underground tunnels. It popped its head above one of its escape routes and then back again as a white owl, returning to the nest from its nocturnal hunt, gave a mellow hoot and glided overhead. Two cottontails appeared from nowhere. Finding one another, they pranced and gave chase until their white scuts disappeared into limestone crannies. Songbirds gave a dawn chorus as they flitted from one tree to the next. High in the pale sky, a gathering of turkey buzzards soared in circles until they spotted the unmoving carcasses, and so began a spiralling descent.

Denim's eyes flickered open. Winged scavengers had surrounded him. He shoved free from the dead wolf. The screeching buzzards hopped away to safety. Dragging himself to the rock pool, he washed the wolf's sticky saliva from his face. Painfully, he bathed the deep wounds on his legs and shoulder. Then he hauled himself to his feet and moved over to the wolf.

Cold green eyes stared blankly; the long tongue lopped out between open jaws. The beast looked formidable in death as when alive. He pulled the dagger out of the animal's flank and, cutting pieces of cloth from his pantaloons, he bandaged his shoulder and legs. Picking up the bag of gold, he limped lamely down the trail and left the buzzards to devour the wolf.

As the rising sun peeped over the hillside, he came across the stallion grazing on berry bushes. Thanking his lucky stars, he pulled himself into the saddle. Every stride of the horse brought him more pain, but he knew he had got to keep riding. If he did not get help soon, he would bleed to death. Burning fever seized his body. He lost all awareness and slumped around the horse's neck. Unaware that its rider was dying, the stallion plodded on relentlessly.

Chapter 11

Young Gus

Denim woke to the sound of curtains flapping in an open window. Except for the locket around his neck and the blanket that covered him, he found himself naked, laying on a wooden bed in a small room. He could smell balsam on the clean bandages that had been applied to the wounds on his legs and shoulder. By the bedside was a pair of boots. Trousers and a shirt were neatly folded on a chair. As he dressed, he picked up the dagger and the bag of gold off the dresser top and left the room.

At the far end of a spacious parlour, a petite, middle-aged woman was banging pots and pans as she busied herself in front of a stove. At a large table sat an elderly man cleaning a handgun.

'Howdy, stranger,' said the old man. He placed the handgun inside a display cabinet and called the woman over.

Denim had already decided that he was in honest people's care when he saw that the bag of gold was intact. 'How long have I been here?' he asked.

'Four days,' said the man.

'Four days!' Denim was shocked.

'Yep, you was close to death, but thanks to my wife's knowledge of medicine, she fixed you up good and proper.'

Embarrassed to know that the woman had stripped him, Denim thanked her for saving his life. 'Oh, and I took the liberty of putting these clothes on.'

'That's what they was put there for,' said the woman directly.

Feeling a bit clumsy, Denim turned to the man. 'Is my horse all right?'

'Yep, it's out back. The stallion must have picked up the spoor of the mares in the corral, and brought you straight here.'

'If I could trouble you for food and water,' said Denim, 'I'll be on my way. I can pay you for them.'

'We wouldn't hear of it,' said the man, turning to his wife. 'Would we?'

'Of course not,' said the wife. Even though Denim had arrived in torn, bloody clothes and bare feet, her intuition told her that he was a good person. She put her hand on her husband's shoulder. 'Now, if the stranger would like to introduce himself, he's welcome to join us for dinner.'

'Oh, I beg your pardon, ma'am, my name is Denim Armstrong and I would be pleased to accept your kind invitation.'

'Then you can call me Mary and this here is Henry,' she said, and went back to the stove.

All three sat at the large table, and Mary served up rabbit stew and homemade bread. As they dined, Henry talked about his early life as a gunsmith, living west of the Pecos, and how he had always fancied farming, so he had purchased this small piece of land near the forest. The cabin had been in need of repair, but there was plenty of timber to hand and, although the ground wanted some heavy tilling, he and Mary were happy with their lot.

While listening to their enthusiasm for the outdoor life, Denim admired the display of guns and rifles on the wall. Eventually, the couple's curiosity focused on Denim's injuries, and they were shocked when he told them about the wolf. After verbal explorations were exhausted, the couple welcomed Denim to stay another night.

Early the next morning, Denim had a strip wash in the water trough outside by the corral, and over breakfast he discussed buying one of the handguns from the display cabinet. Henry was not interested in selling, but he had taken such a liking to the white bone-handled dagger that he offered a straight swap. Denim was loath to part with the weapon that had saved his life, but he had more need of a gun.

Out by the corral, Henry gave Denim directions to the nearest town. 'Go west, toward the Blue Ridge Mountains.' He pointed to the peaks in the distance. 'Ride through the Red Maze Canyon, and then go south. You'll come to Rialto Springs Waterfall. Two miles farther and you'll be in Rialto Town. About five days' ride, in all, I reckon.'

Mary presented Denim with a canteen of water and some dried jerky wrapped in salt cloth. He thanked the couple for their hospitality and, saddling the stallion, he rode away.

'Watch out for the Indians,' Henry hollered. 'I heard that some young buckskins are on the war path.'

'I will,' shouted Denim, and waved. How surprised the couple would be, he thought, when they find the small pile of gold doubloons on the dresser top. It was the least he could do for people who had saved his life.

Two days down the trail, Denim saw a wagon train stretching across the open land. Perhaps they were going to Rialto, he thought, and in need of food and water he rode fast to intercept. A portly man dressed in blue dungarees and sporting a wiry moustache pulled the reins on the lead wagon and stopped the train. Denim introduced himself and asked for directions to the town.

'John Bull is the name,' said the brusque voice, 'and I'm the wagon master of these here homesteaders. And nope, I've not heard of Rialto Town, but you're welcome to ride along with us, if you've a mind to.' He shook the reins and shouted, 'Giddy up!' Four horses strained against the harness and the wagon rolled forward, leading the train onward. John Bull is a man of few words, thought Denim, as he rode down the line and tagged on to the last wagon.

The train of wagons rode steadily across the plains until dusk. Coming to a hillside, where a forest of bushes had taken hold, John Bull shouted orders for the wagons to circle. Horses were unhitched and tied to grazing ropes, while young boys went to collect brushwood. Before long, a large fire was blazing in the middle of the camp and food was cooking. Homesteaders showed their friendliness by inviting Denim to eat with them and, after everyone had satisfied their appetite, the campers indulged in a merry shindig to the sound of the harmonica and the fiddle.

Hours later, when the dancing had stopped and most of the homesteaders had retired for the night, Denim sat around the campfire with the elders, and learned why they were making this long trek into the wilderness. Outlaws and senseless killings had driven them out of their small hamlet and, after employing an experienced wagon master, John Bull, they had packed all their worldly possessions into fifteen wagons and four pull carts to seek fresh pastures and a new start in life. Denim wished them luck in their venture and bid them goodnight. One of the homesteaders offered shelter underneath his wagon, in case of rain, he said.

At daybreak, Denim was awakened by something moving underneath the wagon. Surprised to see a young boy, he spoke sharply. 'What are you doing?'

'Sorry mister, I didn't see you there,' blurted the boy, as he crouched behind one of the wheels. 'I'm playing tag with my friends, and they're trying to find me.'

'What! You're playing games this early in the morning?' Without answering, the boy looked pensively through the spokes of the wagon wheel. 'What's your name, boy?'

'It's Gus,' replied the boy. 'Who are you?'

'Oh, me, I'm just a shipwrecked sailor trying to find his way home,' Denim joshed.

Face full of excitement, Gus spun round. 'Really, mister? Have you really been on a ship? I've never seen the sea, or been on a ship, but I've seen pictures of one in a story book.' How strange, thought Denim. What he had taken for granted, growing up near the docks, this boy had never seen.

Gus was bubbling with enthusiasm. 'I once saw one of the big riverboats sailing down the Mississippi, but never a large ship with sails like the one in my picture book.' Surprised at the boy's interest, Denim showed him how to make sailors' knots from two pieces of rope. The boy's favourite was the reef knot.

'Wow, it looks like a number eight, and that's my age,' said Gus, proudly. 'Can I keep it?'

'Sure,' said Denim.

He took kindly to the boy and went on to tell him tales about beautiful mermaids; winged creatures called Sirens that lured men to their deaths on lonely islands; ghost ships that forever sailed the seas; Blackbeard the pirate; the curse of Captain Kidd's treasure, buried on Oak Island; and the Kraken, a giant sea monster that devoured ships and all the men on them, by pulling them under the ocean. The boy was mesmerized by the incredible stories and would have stayed there all day listening, but his friends finally found his hiding place. 'See you later, mister,' Gus shouted, and ran off to play.

Denim laughed at the boy's gusto, and watched the friends chasing in hot pursuit. The youngsters' high spirits brought back memories of his own childhood days, playing pirates down by the docks. But as usual, whenever he reminisced, homely pictures of his mother, father, two brothers, and his little sister filled his mind. Pushing aside those joyful thoughts, he walked over to one of the small cooking fires where he was offered a plate of hot beans. As he ate, he watched the homesteaders go through their morning rituals: washing, cooking, and harnessing the horses.

An hour later, the fires were dampened and the homesteaders got ready to decamp. Denim filled his canteen from a water barrel on the side of the wagon and saddled his horse. When John Bull shouted from up front, the wagons rolled forward in single file and, like a huge caterpillar, they strung out across the land.

Late afternoon, Denim could see that the homesteaders' route was moving farther away from the Blue Ridge Mountains, so he decided to break from the train. Thanking the families that had been so kind to him, he made a quick search for Gus. Unable to find him, he smiled; the boy's probably in hiding again, he thought. Riding up front to the lead wagon, he greeted John Bull. 'I've come to say thanks and goodbye.'

'So you're going your own way, then,' said John Bull.

'I need to find Rialto Town – and a job.'

'Here,' said the wagon master. He reached inside the wagon and pulled out a small bag of oats and beans. 'For your journey – it's not much, but it will help you on your way.'

'Thanks,' said Denim in surprise. 'It's much appreciated. I hope you find your haven.'

'And I hope you find your town,' laughed the wagon master.

'*Adios*,' shouted Denim, and rode away.

Riding until nightfall, Denim came to a sizeable tree and made camp. Since the wolf attack, he thought it safer to have his back protected. He ate some of the oats and beans that John Bull had given him and then slept. Early morning, he made a start towards the mountains. Midday, he stopped riding to take a drink from the canteen. He turned in the saddle to look back down the trail and to gauge how far he had come. Over the hills, in the direction that the wagon train had taken, he saw plumes of black smoke rising. He remembered Henry's warning about renegade Indians and hoped that Gus and the homesteaders were safe. Perhaps it was just a brush fire, he thought; either way, he could do nothing to help – he was more than a day's ride away. Kicking the stallion onward, he started to cross the flats towards the Blue Ridge Mountains.

Chapter 12

Massacre

As the wagon train continued its pilgrimage across the open prairie, Gus played chase with the boys. Even so, he could not stop thinking about the fantastic sea stories. When all the wagons were circled that evening, he went to find the storyteller. He was crestfallen when he was told the sailor-man had left the wagon train and was not coming back.

Crawling underneath his mother's wagon, where he often played, he took the reef knot out of his pocket and wondered if he would ever see the sailor-man again. Then he thought about the wagon train's destination. He had often heard the womenfolk say that their new home would be a haven with green pastures for rearing cattle, sheep, and other stock; a river to irrigate the crops that they would grow; and woodland to enable them to build log cabins and a schoolhouse. The priority would be to build a church; commandments of the Bible would govern their new community, and everyone would be law abiding and live peaceably.

Gus's interpretation was there would be forests to explore, trees to climb, corn fields to hide in, a river to swim, and fish to catch. A young boy's paradise. It all sounded very exciting, but when would they arrive? How many more days would it take, travelling through this barren wilderness, before they reached the so-called promised land? His thoughts were interrupted when he heard the boys running to collect firewood from a nearby copse. He put the reef knot inside his pocket and went to help his friends.

Before long, a blazing fire was roaring. Gus loved the big campfires. The warmth that glowed as the flames licked high into the dark night was comforting. How homely it all was, he thought, as the fire cast dancing lights on people's faces as they chatted and laughed, relieved at having got through another day without mishap.

The day's catch of rabbit and ptarmigan was stewed in several large cauldrons boiling by the fireside, and then served as a thick broth. Appetites appeased, pots and pans were cleared away and the night became alive with music from the harmonica and the squeezebox. This was the signal for the ladies to put on their best long dresses and to dance in turn to the lively melodies. Eventually, the men joined in with the merriment. And as the fun of the night went on, with songs and laughter around the campfire, Gus and his friends played tag, weaving in and out of the wagons, while the camp dogs gave chase and barked excitedly.

Eventually, he tired of the children's games, and joined the elders to listen to their wonderful tales of Jim Bowie, Kit Carson, and Davy Crockett. He always thrilled at these legendary accounts of the Wild West, even though he had heard the stories many times before.

As the homesteaders partied on into the early hours of morning, sleepiness overcame Gus and he moved over to the loving arms of his mother, who sat by the fireside. She hugged him tightly as he snuggled up to her warm bosom and twirled her beautiful, long locks of red hair. He liked to play with the silver ring on her finger, sometimes slipping it off while she pretended not to know, and then sliding it back onto another finger, much to her exaggerated surprise. It was all good fun to Gus.

Although he had never known his father, he was happy and content. His mother had always been there for all of his needs, and she meant the world to him. As he rested his head on her lap and gazed at the warm glowing fire, she stroked his tousled hair. He felt safe and secure. What a joy it all was, he thought. With his mother's silver ring clenched tightly in his fist, he fell into deep slumber.

Gus awoke to the stench of smoke and birds cawing loudly. Half awake, he lay there in a dreamy state trying to understand the smells and noises. He rubbed the sleep from his eyes and sat upright. Hot blood coursed down his face. He cried out for his mother, but there was no answer. No caring arms reached out to comfort him. No warm bosom snuggled him tight. Instead of a soft voice to soothe his fears, a dull pain thumped inside his head.

Using his shirt sleeve, he wiped the blood from his face. The sight that came to his eyes terrified him. All the wagons had been overturned; some were on fire. Homesteaders' belongings were scattered about the camp. Dead bodies lay everywhere. Vultures screeched and squabbled over pieces of flesh, as they hopped from one cadaver to the next. Flocks of carrion crows kept their distance from the large scavengers, and waited their turn for an orgy of feasting.

Gus tried to stand. A body was lying across his legs. He pushed free. As the body rolled over he screamed out in shock. His mother's eyes were wide open in a deathly gaze. Her scalp was bloody, the long locks of red hair missing. He shouted for her to speak. The silence made him shudder in fear. He dropped to his knees and cradled her lifeless body in his arms. Then, rocking backwards and forwards, he wailed his grief to the heavens. Occasionally, he glanced at the other bodies being ripped apart, then he would hold on all the more tightly to his mother, as if to protect her. All day and night he nursed his mother until falling asleep.

Dawn light was strong. He opened his eyes. The nightmare was still there. Swarms of flies buzzed over decomposing bodies. Vultures had long since flown, but now carrion crows pecked at the remains. He looked at the silver ring in his hand, and clenched it more tightly. Thirst and hunger forced him to leave his mother's side. As he stood upright, blood trickled from the wound on his head. Trance-like, he wandered through the camp. All the horses were gone. Any food that had been left had been destroyed along with the burned-out wagons. He came across one of the camp dogs lying on the ground. Its legs were outstretched as if still running from the onslaught. Two arrows protruded from its flank.

In a daze and having no sense of direction, he left the circle of smoking ashes far behind. As he stumbled away from the brutal massacre, he sobbed repeatedly. 'It was Injuns, they did it. They killed my Ma. One day, I will kill 'em. I'll kill them all.'

The heat of the relentless sun brought him falling to his knees. Lips cracked and tongue swollen, he panted hard for breath. Unable to go any further, he sagged to the ground. For a while he lay there, eyes closed. Then he heard the faint sound of trickling water. He raised his head to look. The sun was blinding. He tried to crawl forward. Too weak to move, he collapsed face down into the dirt.

Crystal-clear waters played a melodious tune as they rippled over cobbles of stone and meandered lazily across the dry landscape. A waterfowl gave a solitary high-pitched call and then disappeared into an oasis of lush, green foliage. Swifts darted here and there, catching insects in the air. Flying high and then low, they dipped their wings as they skimmed the shallow river. Only feet away from the limpid, cool waters, the frail body of a lonely boy lay dying. His little fist was still clenched tight.

Chapter 13

The Desperado

From the top of the plateau, deep-set eyes looked through an old pair of army-issue field glasses and scanned the escape route up the mountain. The posse had not followed him. He lit a cheroot and inhaled deeply. Then he looked in the direction of the town in the north, where three days ago he had killed two men in a gunfight. Five miles south was his next destination: Rialto Town. A cloud of dust in the east made him shift his viewpoint. A lone black stallion was crossing the flatlands. Could be a lawman, he thought, but the rider was too far away to tell. Folding the glasses, he placed them inside the saddlebag strapped to the rump of a golden palomino.

Strong winds made him snuggle the Spanish black hat down on his head. Silver coins on the hatband flashed in the sun. He drew in heavily on the cheroot before throwing the nub to the ground and stubbing it out with the heel of his black boot. For three days he had ridden hard to escape the posse; now he was hungry. The desperado pulled the Spencer repeating rifle out of its scabbard and mounted the palomino.

Game was scarce on the mountain, but before nightfall he had bagged a jack rabbit with a single shot. Finding shelter among the rocks, he shackled the horse's front legs together and then built a fire. After roasting the meat, he picked the bones clean, then he unbuckled the shiny black gun from around his waist and laid it across his lap. As he rested against a large rock, he rubbed the half-moon scar on his right cheek and gazed at the myriad of stars. From somewhere in the isolated ravines below he heard the woeful cry of a coyote. Moments later, a haunting reply echoed through the mountain tops.

Entranced by the glow of the firelight, he reminisced of the day when a saddle tramp had ridden into his home town and had given him the gun. At sixteen years of age he had thought how lucky he was, but after taking ownership, an inexplicable euphoria compelled him into a life of crime. Quick on the draw, he soon gained the reputation of 'Top Gun'. His fiancée, family, and friends forsake him as he became wanted by the law.

He blamed the gun for his moral decline and, believing it was cursed, he dubbed it the Devil Gun. Often, he had thought about getting rid of it, but that was easier said than done. For whenever he killed someone, the feeling of supremacy that surged through his body had always made him keep possession. Now, after being on the run for thirty years, he wanted a better life: he had to give up the Devil Gun.

As he gazed at the flickering campfire, he caught sight of movement in the shadows. A sidewinder slithered out of a rocky crevice and glided silently towards him. He kept very still. The snake raised its head. Its tail rattled. Faster than a dart, it struck. The gun flew into his hand. Two shots echoed across the mountain. Head severed, the reptile writhed upon the dirt.

Tingling sensations played up the desperado's arm. A warm glow surged through his body. He felt good. For years, people had marvelled at his prowess, but he owed the speed and accuracy to the Devil Gun. It was as if it had a life of its own. He knew that while he had possession, he was invincible. However, he always feared the day when the gun might lose its strange power. He kissed the small rabbit's foot dangling on the silver chain attached to his shirt button for good luck, and pulling the Spanish hat over his eyes, he dozed.

A high-pitched screech awoke him. He grabbed the gun. A hawk swooped out of the early morning sky and snatched a small rodent. As the predator flew away with its quarry, the desperado eased the trigger. High in the grey sky, a pair of black condors soared gracefully. He watched them for a while until the scream of a cougar, some way off on the mountain slopes, stirred him.

Poking the ashes of the burned-out fire, he provoked new flames and fed them sticks. Using a small penknife, he skinned and diced the dead snake and toasted the cubes of flesh. After eating his fill, he put out the fire, released the shackles on the palomino, and found another route down the mountain. Gently kicking his horse, he rode off in the direction of Rialto Town.

Denim had heard the gunshots from the plateau, and guessed that someone was hunting. But now, as daylight was fast fading, he bedded down for the night. The next morning he continued his trek across the sandy flatlands, but it was slow going. It took all day to reach the base of the mountains, and the best part of another day before he found the entrance to the Red Maze Canyon. Deciding it would be safer to find his way through the canyon in daylight, he made camp. That night he ate the last of the beans and oats that John Bull had given him.

Chapter 14

Davy's Story

The year 1861 had been a very good one for Rialto Town. More than twenty Mormon families had settled in the adjoining neighbourhood and businesses had flourished, leading to the building of a new church school which became the pride of the community. Although the townsfolk readily accepted the new-found wealth that the Mormons had brought to their community, they wanted segregation too, and were content when the religious sect built a settlement two miles east of town, on the edge of a dense forest.

Joshua John Morton, a devout Mormon, was moving his family to the settlement. Disciplined and solemn, he sat tall in the open buckboard that carried food supplies and belongings. Bearded down to his chest and wearing a tall black hat akin to Abraham Lincoln's, he cracked a small stick-whip above the team of horses, and led the way for his four wives in the wagon that trailed.

Dressed in poke bonnets, three wives pacified their family of nine children under the canvas hoops, while Elizabeth, who was the eldest of the women, drove the wagon. Eager to get to their destination, the family rode into the busy town and asked directions to the Mormon camp.

Young Davy lifted the canvas covering on mother's wagon and peeked out. He spied the church school and pulled a face of dislike. At ten years of age he would be expected to attend. He hoped the community would be friendlier than in previous towns, for the hostility towards Mormons had always forced them to move on, and he was beginning to wonder if his father would ever find an ideal place for them to settle.

Taking direction from one of the townsfolk, Davy's father led the way due east towards the Mormon settlement. On arrival they were welcomed by other religious squatters and, within days, a sizeable cabin had been built with logs hewn from the nearby forest. With only two bedrooms and one large living room to house his father, six elder sisters, and two younger brothers – along with the four wives – Davy thought life was a bit crowded.

As soon as the new church was open for service, Davy was sent, against his wishes, to attend school there. Other Mormon families decided to wait until their own church school had been built, rather than send their children into town, but Davy's father insisted that his son should attend. His sisters did not need educating, according to father, and his brothers were too young; Davy went to school alone.

Walking two miles along the edge of the forest to attend class six days a week in Rialto Town, became an unforgettable chore to Davy. After several weeks of the trudge, he started to loathe school and the tutor along with it. The tutor's name, Slim Theakstone, was always a source of amusement to young Davy, for the man was small, fat, and bald headed. With two beady eyes staring through wire-framed spectacles, which always looked as if they were about to drop off his stubby nose, he reminded Davy of a barn owl.

Slim Theakstone was a faithful Christian and although he hated Mormons he could not be seen to discriminate against any new pupil. The fear of the town's select committee removing him from office was always a deterrent, hence Davy was admitted into class. Theakstone was a learned man by all accounts, but by no means was he a teacher. His rules were strict and the children learned lessons by fear, rather than face the wrath of Theakstone.

Davy soon learned that the 'Theakstone Wrath', as the children called it, was a punishment to avoid at all costs. Any misbehaving child would have their shoes and socks removed and, while other children held the offender down, a beating on the soles of their bare feet, with a cane, would be vigorously undertaken by the tutor.

After suffering the Theakstone Wrath twice during the first weeks at school, Davy soon came to despise the man behind the stick, who seemed to get great pleasure from doling out this cruel form of punishment.

Small in stature, Davy was the only Mormon in class, and he was instantly disliked by Theakstone, who often humiliated him by calling him 'Little Runt'. This nickname was readily undertaken by the other pupils and whenever they tormented him, it would be Davy who was singled out as the offender and punished by the tutor. On top of that, he had to face the school bully, Seth Crapper, who was better known as Scrapper. He was the tallest boy in class, and his favourite pastime was to intimidate Davy.

Davy's life was made even more miserable by his bad-tempered father, who often beat him for the slightest mishap. And whenever Davy was sent on errands in town, he was beset upon by the older boys that lived there. Every time he fought back, he lost. He often thought about running away from home, but with a life experience of how horrible people could be, he doubted that he would survive long anywhere else.

After suffering four long weeks at school, something unusual happened in Rialto that unnerved the whole community. A mysterious stranger on a golden palomino rode into town. The townsfolk were always curious about newcomers, but this man was different to any that had ever visited before. With brutal arrogance he demanded everything, from food and drink to a room in which to stay and, much to Davy's amazement, everything was provided – and without payment. Everyone cowered in this man's presence.

Davy could not make sense of it all, until he was sent to the general store in town. While waiting to collect a small parcel of herbs for one of the mothers, he was privy to the conversation between the storekeeper and two customers.

'They say the stranger is a bounty hunter,' said the storekeeper, 'and he will kill anyone for money.'

The unshaven customer picked up a large bag of flour, threw it onto his shoulder, and scoffed, 'Huh, if Billy Briscoe had been here, he would have run the bounty hunter out of town,'

A smartly dressed man stopped thumbing through a clothes catalogue on the counter and retorted, 'Billy Briscoe! Why, he's nothing but a braggart. He wouldn't stand a chance against the likes of this killer.'

'I don't know about that,' interrupted the store-keeper, 'Billy Briscoe's pretty slick with a gun. He wins all the shooting competitions around here.'

'It's easy to shoot at targets,' claimed the smartly dressed man. 'They don't shoot back.'

The unshaven man paid for the bag of flour and snapped, 'Billy Briscoe would have booted the stranger out of town before you could say "Stonewall

Jackson". You could bet your bottom dollar on that!'

'I reckon you're right,' said the storekeeper, picking the money up off the counter. 'Billy Briscoe would have sorted him.'

The smartly dressed man sneered at the two men's alliance and lit a large cigar. As the conversation broadened, Davy learned that the town was dependent on the County US Marshal, who visited once every three months. In the meantime the local hothead, Billy Briscoe, took it upon himself to enforce the law.

Puffing heavily on the cigar, the smartly dressed man stated, 'I've campaigned to get a sheriff elected for the last two years in this town, but no one pays any heed. That leaves killers like this one free to break the law and come and go as they please. And there's nobody in town brave enough, or good enough, to stop him.'

'How about you stopping him, then?' laughed the unshaven man, as he left the store with the bag of flour on his shoulder.

'It's not my job!' shouted the smartly dressed man, choking on the cigar. He turned to the storekeeper and emphasized his point. 'This town needs a sheriff!'

Finally, the storekeeper noticed Davy waiting and handed him the small parcel of herbs. On his way home, Davy thought about the bounty hunter. The name conjured up a heroic figure as he recalled stories of how they tracked down and killed the toughest of outlaws for reward money.

The next day, while walking to school, Davy saw the stranger leave the hardware store and ride out of town. Deciding to skip class, Davy followed the rider. Weeks of being chased by the boys in town had made him fleet of foot, and two miles down the trail he caught up with the palomino, tethered at the waterfall.

Hiding behind a prickly furze bush, he watched the stranger place several small rocks on top of a large boulder, then retreat a number of paces to fire his gun. One by one, the rocks exploded into tiny pieces. Enchanted by the shooting display, Davy accidentally wandered out of his hiding place and, like the snake that is musically charmed out of its basket, he found he had moved closer than he had intended.

The gunman had been aware of the boy's presence all along and beckoned him over. Davy did not move. The man laughed at the boy's caution and set about placing more rocks on top of the boulder. Reassured by the laughter, Davy came closer. He could see the half-moon scar on the man's face and the small rabbit's foot dangling on a chain from his shirt. Silver coins on the Spanish black hat sparkled in the morning sun. Davy had never seen anything so fancy on a man before.

'Have you ever fired a gun, sonny?' the gravel voice asked.

'No, sir,' Davy gulped. And he was surprised when the stranger offered him the shiny black gun.

'Go on, try your luck,' said the stranger, pointing at the boulder.

The gun was heavy and awkward. Davy pulled hard on the trigger. The violent explosion jerked his hand upward. Dust scattered into the air yards short of the boulder. Reclaiming the gun, the stranger holstered it and then swiftly, drew the weapon and fired. One of the rocks exploded. With a twirl of his fingers the gun glided back inside the holster and then out again, faster than before. Fanning the trigger hammer with his left hand, three more rocks shattered into the air.

Davy's eyes opened wide. He blew a whistle of air

through his teeth. 'Gosh, mister, that was great.'

The man smiled at the young boy's thrill. He had spotted him the day before, through the bedroom window of the hardware store, where he had watched a gang of kids chase and throw stones at him. The boy needed a gun, thought the stranger. Reloading the firearm, he handed it over and gave advice. 'Remember this, sonny: if you're good enough, you only need one gun. Practice is the secret. Always grip the handle firmly. Point the barrel at your target, just as you would point your finger at someone. Stare without blinking and hold your breath as you fire. Squeeze the trigger, don't pull.'

Davy tried his hardest to put the instructions into practice, but he did not even hit the large boulder, and he doubted that he would ever be able to score a target. Yet he was enthralled at having fired the gun and yearned to have another go. The stranger took possession of the gun and climbed into the saddle. Seeing the boy's disappointment, he offered him some hope. 'If you're close enough, and the target is big enough, you don't need to aim – you can't miss.' He kicked the palomino into a canter, and rode off in the direction of town.

As the stranger rode out of sight, Davy pretended he was holding the shiny black gun. He went through the motions: point... hold your breath... squeeze the trigger. His aim was perfect. Every shot hit the target. Each rock exploded into dust. Eventually, he tired of this makeshift game and sat by the waterfall. He wondered why everyone in town was afraid of the stranger, the only person who had shown Davy any kindness. Playing by the pool, he tried to catch fish with a piece of string until it was time for the school to turn out. He knew he had to arrive home as if he had attended class, or he would receive another thrashing from his father.

Davy arrived home on time, and with no questions asked of his whereabouts during the day, he sat at the dining table in the cabin. One of the mothers served him bread and broth and, after completing his daily chores – chopping firewood, feeding the horses, and cleaning the wagons – he retired to the bedroom. Going to the opposite corner to where his brothers and sisters slept, he lay on the floor and covered himself with a blanket.

Next day, being the Sabbath, Davy was sent into town, as usual, with a shopping list. As he bypassed the church, he heard the congregation in full song. At the hardware store there was an air of excitement; a large crowd had gathered outside. He popped the shopping list into the mail box outside the store and mingled among the people. News was, that Billy Briscoe was back, and that he had sent a warning to the stranger to get out of town before noon.

As the church bells clanged midday, Davy moved to the sidewalk opposite the store, to get a better view of the impending fight. Suddenly, the crowd parted. A young man, shirt sleeves rolled back at the cuffs, gun strapped neatly at his side, stood alone, straight-legged, and facing the store. When the bounty hunter appeared in the shop doorway, the crowds took a nervous step backward. Carrying two saddlebags, he walked over to the palomino at the hitching rail and strapped them on the horse's rump.

The bounty hunter is on the run, thought Billy Briscoe. Chest inflating with confidence, he shouted a brash warning. 'It's midday, mister, and you haven't left town!' Billy Briscoe's hand hovered over his gun.

Without saying a word, the stranger tightened the cinch around the horse's girth and climbed onto the saddle. With a gentle kick, the palomino broke out into a trot. Outraged at being ignored, Billy Briscoe drew his gun.

'Stop him! He's robbed the tills.' Dishevelled and bleeding, the storekeeper staggered out of the shop doorway and aimed a rifle at the stranger's back. People ran for cover.

'Look out, mister!' yelled Davy.

Before the warning words had died on the wind, the bounty hunter had dived off the horse and had fired two shots. Billy Briscoe crumpled to the ground. The storekeeper was sent crashing through the shop window. Jumping to his feet, the bounty hunter quickly reloaded. A shrill whistle brought the palomino trotting to his side. He climbed aloft and turned the horse in the direction of Davy on the sidewalk.

Davy wanted to run away, but his legs would not move. The palomino came so close that he could feel the hot air blowing down its nostrils. Leaning over in the saddle the bounty hunter prodded the gun into Davy's belly. Words echoed in Davy's mind: *If you're close enough, and the target is big enough, you don't need to aim – you can't miss.* Davy's heart skipped a beat; he knew he was about to die.

A sudden flick of the wrist and the bounty hunter was holding the barrel of the gun. He pushed the handle towards Davy. 'Take it,' said the gruff voice. Davy dared not move. The gravel voice deepened. 'Take it. It's yours.'

Nervously, Davy took hold of the gun and the palomino backed away. The stranger remembered the black stallion he had seen crossing the flats to the mountain. If the rider was a lawman, he would soon be arriving in Rialto Town. Without the black shiny gun he knew he was vulnerable. It was time to move on.

Slowly, the townsfolk came out of hiding, and watched the stranger ride out of town. They would never know who he was, where he was going or where he had come from. Davy stuffed the gun inside his shirt and ran off in the direction of home. Entering the forest, he sat at the bole of a lofty cedar to examine the gun; six bullets. He aimed at the birds in the treetops, then he decided not to waste the ammunition; it might be difficult to get more. Overwhelmed with excitement, he did not feel the strange tingling sensations up his arm or the warm glow of the gun. Ripping a strip of cloth off the bottom of his shirt, he wrapped it tightly around the six-shooter, and buried it at the root of the tree. This was his secret, and he felt good about it.

Billy Briscoe's funeral, and that of the storekeeper, came and went, but the townsfolk blamed the death of their two citizens on Davy and so treated his father with contempt. In turn, Davy was thrashed for bringing shame upon the family. At school, he was shunned by the pupils as they took up the town's sentiments. On top of that, Scrapper continually mocked him for warning the stranger.

Assembling in the school courtyard, Davy noticed that Scrapper was in one of his sullen staring moods. The stare had always preceded an attack, but this time Davy took the initiative and ran headlong into Scrapper's face. Taken by surprise, Scrapper clung onto Davy as they fell. Gouging and clawing at one another, they rolled across the ground. The pupils quickly circled and yelled encouragement.

Slim Theakstone was waiting for the children to arrive in class, but when he heard the fracas outside he came to investigate. He shoved his way through the noisy spectators and drenched the two boys with a pail of water. 'Stand up! Both of you,' he demanded.

Soaking wet, the two boys struggled to their feet. Expecting the Theakstone Wrath to be administered, the pupils wondered what was going to happen when the tutor grabbed both boys by the scruff of the neck and made them stand face to face.

'So you want to fight, do you?' said Theakstone. 'We will soon sort this out. Hold out your left hand, both of you.' Producing a large neckerchief from his pocket, he knotted the boy's wrists together. 'If you want to fight, then so be it. This will make sure that neither of you can run away.'

Pushing and pulling, sometimes kicking, the two boys began to battle. Davy landed blows to Scrapper's torso, while Scrapper, being taller, hit Davy repeatedly in the face. Screaming excitedly, the pupils shouted for each boy to do their worst. Theakstone smirked with satisfaction as he watched the Mormon boy take a beating. Continual punches to the face became too much for Davy. Bruised and bleeding, he dropped to the ground and curled into a ball. Scrapper threw punches at will until he ran out of steam and sagged to his knees.

Dismayed that the fight was over, Slim Theakstone untied the neckerchief that bound the two boys, and slung it in Davy's face. 'Let that be a lesson to you, you Little Runt,' he scowled, wagging his finger. Then he grabbed Scrapper by the ear and pushed him and the other pupils indoors, leaving Davy battered and bleeding on the ground.

Coughing and spitting blood, Davy lay there thinking the whole world was against him. Downcast and in pain, he dabbed his bloody and swollen face with the neckerchief. His clothes were ripped and stained with blood; he knew if he arrived at home in this state, he would get another beating. But there was nowhere else to go; what could he do? Body shaking in distress, he started to weep. At length he dragged himself together and began the slow trek home.

Vile thoughts of revenge clouded his mind. He hated the kids who constantly taunted him, and the bully boy who had antagonized him since the first day at school. He loathed the tutor, who had chastised and punished him at every opportunity. And the townsfolk, who had made him a social outcast. He was disgusted with the four mothers who had never come to his aid, whenever father was thrashing him, and he disliked his brothers and sisters who had never once consoled him. But most of all, he detested his father, who had shown nothing but contempt for him since the day he had been born.

Arriving at the forest, Davy found his favourite tree and slumped beside it. A quiet moment passed as he relived the humiliations he had just suffered. Then, he cushioned his beaten face in his hands and wept uncontrollably. He sobbed until a loud wailing lament escaped his bloody swollen lips, and the sadness of his life echoed throughout the lonely woodland.

Hours later, he awoke in a darkened forest where the sunlight was fast fading. School would be closing shortly. He must get home in time – as if he had attended class. As he rose to his feet, pain dropped him onto his knees. For some time he remained there, caressing his battered face, then as if possessed by some evil spirit, he began to claw frantically at the soil. His facial wounds throbbed from the exertion. Fresh blood dripped to the ground.

The hidden bundle came to the surface. He ripped the shirt cloth away and let it drop to the ground. He gripped the gun. A warm glow surged through his body. Tingling sensations moved up his arm. He felt good. For the first time in his life he felt confident. He checked the firing chamber; it was fully loaded. A faint smile stung his torn lips as he recalled the stranger's advice: *If you're close enough, and the target is big enough, you don't need to aim – you can't miss.*

Evil thoughts raced through his mind as religious doctrine, an eye for an eye, sanctioned his plans for revenge. He jumped to his feet. This time he was oblivious to his pains. Now he had a purpose. A reason to live. It was time to get even.

Chapter 15

The Reckoning

Since the death of its two citizens, the goodwill of the town towards the religious settlers was lost and Slim Theakstone now felt free to show his prejudices. He had never wanted the Mormon boy in his class from the start and, although the Little Runt had not attended lessons since the morning fight, he was not concerned. He hoped that would be the last he would ever see of the boy.

Sitting at a tall writing desk next to a half-open window, Slim Theakstone thought how peaceful it was as the children, sitting in rows at small wooden tables, went through the motions of silent reading. He gave a retiring sigh and paused the letter he was writing. Taking the Henry Pitkin watch out of the fob pocket on his waistcoat, he looked at the time. Ten minutes to go before the end of class. He was looking forward to going home and preparing dinner. Cooking was his favourite pastime and, after living alone all these years, he had become quite the connoisseur. He had never married, for he had no interest in women and – though his job belied the fact – he hated children.

Although he wanted to complete the letter before the end of class, he could not help daydreaming as he gazed out of the window and watched finches going through their courting rituals in the nearby bushes. Beyond the shrubbery and in the distance, he could see the forest where rich swathes of colourful sprouting leaves displayed the onset of spring. High above the woodlands, a large flock of Canada geese trailed in a long V-formation as they squawked their way across the fast-fading blue sky. Soft breezes through the half-open window carried the aroma of wild flowers growing in the nearby pastures. It gave him cause to stretch his arms and take in a deep breath. Oh for the beauty of it all. Life was glorious, he thought, as he marvelled at the wonders of nature.

He gave another long, contented sigh; the sun was shining, the birds were singing, and the weekend looked promising. Perhaps he would visit his sister in the next town, or do a spot of fishing at the waterfall. He took the timepiece out again. Only five minutes more – he must finish the letter. Returning the watch to the fob pocket, he resumed writing.

Suddenly, the classroom door banged wide open. The pupils gasped in shock. Davy, bloodied and ragged, pointed a gun. Boom! The blast lifted Scrapper out of his chair and onto the table behind. Blood poured from a hole in his chest. Panic stricken, the pupils scrambled through a second door, to escape.

'Stop this nonsense at once, boy!' Slim Theakstone screamed his authority.

Another deafening roar filled the room. The half-open window next to Theakstone shattered into tiny pieces. Davy began to panic – the shot had missed. Then the words came to him strongly: *If you're close enough, and the target is big enough, you don't need to aim – you can't miss.* As if in a trance, Davy closed in on the tutor.

Icy cold shivers ran down Theakstone's spine. Sweat coursed down his chubby face. The spectacles dropped off his stubby nose. Trapped in the corner of the room, there was no escape. He dropped onto his knees and pleaded for mercy. 'No Davy, please don't do it. Please don't kill me.'

The thunderous roar of red flames slammed the tutor sideways. Sprawled across the floor, blood gurgled from his neck. Davy stared at the inert body. This was the man who all the children had obeyed without question. Why had they all been so afraid of him? Look at him now, he's nothing... Nothing! He pulled the trigger again. Theakstone's body gave a spasmodic jerk and then became still. Strong sensations coursed through Davy. He was a god. He had the power to let people live or die. A gust of wind, through the broken window, blew piles of writing paper off the tutor's desk. As they scattered to the floor they covered the mask of death that had once been Slim Theakstone.

Alerted by the gunshots, the townsfolk came running. Davy made a quick exit from the school. He ran as fast as he could across the meadow and into the forest. Reaching the large cedar tree, he dropped beside it. His heart beat fast as he caught his breath. It was like a weird dream: everything had been so easy. He picked up the shirt cloth, which he had left on the ground, and wrapped it around the gun. For his next plan to work he needed to conceal the weapon. There was no time to lose. He knew a lynch mob would come searching for him. He ran off in the direction of home.

In what little daylight was left, he could see the four mothers collecting the washing from string lines stretched between the trees. His sisters were busy tending the vegetable patch; his two young brothers played swing on a rope that dangled from the highest branch. Davy flattened his hair over his face to hide the bruises; then, with his head held low, he walked swiftly towards the cabin door.

From the clothes line, Elizabeth spotted Davy and shouted, 'Davy, your father's sleeping. He must not be disturbed.'

Davy waved the cloth bundle. 'I have something important for my father, and if I don't give it to him straight away he will be very angry.'

Elizabeth had always felt guilty for her son's sad life. She had never admitted her infidelity to her husband, but she knew that Joshua had always suspected Davy was not his child. Whenever her son had taking a beating, she had always been too afraid to intervene because of her husband's violence. And she knew that if her son did not do exactly as father had told him, then he would suffer another thrashing. 'OK Davy, but please be quiet,' said Elizabeth.

Davy took a deep breath to calm his nerves and tiptoed to his father's bedroom. Cautiously, he peered inside. Cloth sacking had been drawn across the window to darken the room, but a small glowing candle on a bedside chair showed father asleep on the bed. Davy let the shirt cloth drop to the floor and aimed the gun. Doubts entered his mind. What if he missed? His first shot had missed Slim Theakstone. Creeping closer he stopped an arm's length away, lest his father should awaken, and pointed the gun.

In the mellow light of the room, the age lines on his father's face had evened out. His dark tormented looks were gone. He looked young and peaceful, almost angelic. Conflicting emotions made Davy hesitate. There was still a deep-seated yearning in his heart to win his father's love. Back in the forest his plans for revenge had seemed simple, but now they were proving hard to execute. He lowered the gun.

As he stood there in the quietness of the room, odious memories seeped into his mind: of being locked in a rat-ridden cellar for days with little food or water; of all the thrashings he had suffered with the leather belt; of the terrifying day when his drunken father had almost drowned him in a nearby river; and of all the times he had cried himself to sleep, trying to understand why his father disliked him so. Tears ran down Davy's cheeks. He felt so unloved. What had he done to deserve such a wretched existence?

Tingling sensations moved up Davy's arm. A warm glow surged through his body, driving out all the self-pity. His fears evaporated as the bounty hunter's words repeated themselves: *If you're close enough, and the target is big enough, you don't need to aim – you can't miss.* Davy pushed the nuzzle of the gun so close that it almost touched his father's face, then he whispered, 'Father... Father.' He wanted his father to see who was about to kill him.

Joshua opened his eyes. For a dreamy moment he did not know where he was. 'Davy...?' he murmured, 'What are you doing here?' Then his eyes opened wide in terror. Davy's nervous fingers twitched on the trigger. Bang! Blood, skin and bone, splattered everywhere. The look of death on his father's face, imprinted onto Davy's mind. He pushed by Elizabeth who had come running. Her horrendous screams awakened the camp. Davy raced to the corral and sprang onto a horse. As he galloped away, Mormon families shouted angrily and fired their guns at him.

Wiping his father's blood from his face, Davy lashed the horse with the reins. He was elated – he had finally killed the man who had made his life a misery. At last, he was fighting back – and winning. Things would be different from now on. There was one bullet left, and that was all he needed to get more. With those reassuring thoughts, he kicked the horse in the direction of Rialto Town Waterfall and the Blue Ridge Mountains. He was born again. A new life awaited him.

Chapter 16

Two Gun Pete

Denim was pleased he had waited until daylight to enter the Red Maze Canyon. Finding a way through was trickier than he had thought. He came to many dead ends where the rocky walls had closed in; and more than once he had to backtrack. Eventually he found his way through the canyon and turned south. As the sun lowered and the evening became cooler, he finally arrived at Rialto Springs Waterfall.

After watering the black stallion and securing it to a thicket, he filled his canteen and quenched his own thirst. Then he sat against a large boulder, and admired the view. The rich crimson sunset silhouetted the mountains and gave a mystical pink hue to the steam of the waterfall as it cascaded down fifty feet of rocky outcrop into a large pool. Glows of fireflies sequinned the surrounding bushes, while distinct trills of unseen crickets chorused against the rasping mating calls of bullfrogs. In the picturesque setting, the melodic sound of gurgling waters soon soothed Denim into sleep.

Denim awoke with a start. Galloping hooves were almost upon him. He jumped to his feet and dived out of the way. A boy rider charged by at breakneck speed. As the horse disappeared into the night, Denim shouted his curses. Then he waited awhile to see if anyone was following. Settling back against the boulder, he wondered what a boy was doing out here, at this time of night.

Early the next morning, the pool looked so inviting

that he stripped down to Henry's old boots and waded in. Feeling refreshed, he dressed and rode off in search of Rialto Town. Before long, he was passing the new church school and riding down a busy main street. He greeted several townsfolk, but they only returned suspicious looks. Coming to a large livery stable that had open doors, Denim waved for attention. An old man stopped grooming horses and came over. 'What can I do for you, stranger?' he asked.

'Water and feed the horse for the night,' said Denim. 'How much?'

Stroking his bushy beard, the old man looked at the stranger's shabby clothes. 'One dollar,' he said, 'if you can pay up front?' Denim dismounted and paid with a gold doubloon.

Through habit, the old man bit the coin to see if it was genuine, and then slid it into his leather apron pocket. 'Staying in town long?'

'Maybe,' said Denim, 'but the townsfolk don't seem very friendly.'

'Haw, pay no heed to them. They're just edgy that's all. Two citizens were shot down, two days ago, in front of the whole town. On the Sabbath, of all days. It was pretty gruesome. Some say the killer was Curly Bill the outlaw, and others say it was a bounty hunter. Whoever he was, he was pretty slick with a gun. He outdrew Billy Briscoe and he was the town's best marksman.'

The old man returned to grooming the horses, but all the while he carried on trumpeting the local news. 'On top of that killing, one of them Mormon boys from the settlement shot dead his teacher and one of the school kids. Happened in the church school of all places.' He shook his head in disgust and eyed the stranger for some reaction, but there was none, so he carried on with the news. 'Then he went and murdered his own father. Yep, while his father was sleeping, he blew his head off. They reckon there was blood everywhere. Some of the townsfolk gave chase but the boy escaped on horseback. The boy hadn't been living here long. I'll tell you this; I wouldn't trust those Mormons as far as I could…'

Realizing the man was an incessant talker, Denim interrupted. 'When did all this happen?'

'Last night!' said the old man curtly. 'Some of the townsfolk went after the boy but by the time...'

'Did they catch him?'

'No! Damn it. But half the town was out all night searching for him.' Not liking interruptions, the old man's bushy eyebrows rose in annoyance. Telling the latest gossip to customers was his pleasure.

Denim assumed it was the same boy who had almost trampled him to death at the waterfall, but he did not say as much and, before the old man could say any more, he asked if there were any jobs in town. The old man was not enamoured of this impatient stranger, but he did need some help. He stroked his bushy beard in thought. 'If you're not opposed to mucking out stables and spreading straw; can't pay much, but you can bed down in the hayloft if that suits.' Before Denim could answer, the man started to rattle out more news. 'Yep, a religious boy at that. You just don't know where you stand with them Mormons. There's over a hundred of them here now, living on the settlement by the forest, and I've always said, you couldn't trust one as far as you could sling a bobcat, and...'

Denim interrupted again. 'I'd like to take you up on that job.'

The old man widened his eyes in surprise, and then stroked his bushy beard. 'Yep, that's OK with me. You can call me Gabby. That's what most folks around here call me, anyways.'

Denim smiled at the aptness of the name, and introduced himself with a handshake. 'Where could a man find something to eat around here, Gabby?'

'Halfway down Main Street. Go past the saloon and you'll find Blanche's Kitchen. The grub's not great, but if you're starving, it's wonderful.' He chortled at his little joke, and then went back to working the horses.

Denim found Blanche's Kitchen and, after making it known that he was working for Gabby, he received a warm welcome and ate a hearty breakfast. Returning to the livery, he cleaned out all the stables before retiring to the hayloft. Next day, he went into town and, with the last pieces of the captain's gold, he purchased a rifle, boots, jacket and jeans, and a Stetson.

Over the coming months he learned how to tend horses: grooming, shoeing, and trimming hooves. In his free time, he practised target shooting and the quick draw. Often, Gabby would read aloud the latest news. The eastern newspapers had coined the boy killer 'Kid Rio' and, although his face was displayed on wanted posters throughout the county, he was never captured.

Winter came and went in Rialto Town and as the spring nights lengthened into summer, Denim got the urge to explore more of this new country. Owning a rifle, he knew he could survive the distance between towns, as there was plenty of wild game out there. He collected some food provisions and, after saying farewell to Gabby and a few other acquaintances, he left Rialto Town.

Crossing the counties from Virginia to Kentucky, Denim fell in with a team of wranglers capturing wild horses in mountain pastures. After months of busting broncos for a living, he moved on to Missouri, and he was pleased to get back to some kind of civilization when he came upon Jackson Town.

Riding by the shacks and lean-tos that made up the town, Denim wondered where all the people were until he saw faces peering at him from behind curtained windows. He tethered his horse outside the Gold Nugget Saloon and entered. At the far end of the room, four men were sat at a table, next to the wall. Denim asked the middle-aged barman for a beer, and tossed a dollar onto the counter. The portly man filled a glass and shoved it across the bar. Then, looking around nervously, he whispered, 'If I were you, mister, I'd leave now while you've still got the chance.'

Denim took a large gulp of beer. He had no intention of leaving yet. 'Why, what's going on?'

The barman nodded in the direction of the four men. 'One of them is Ben Adams. He's a fast gun from hereabouts and...'

'Whiskey!' growled a voice.

The barman snatched a bottle of whiskey from the shelf and ran to the table at the end of the room. A big ugly man dressed in a black frock coat grabbed the bottle and poured drinks for himself and his three friends.

Returning to the bar, the barman spoke again, in a low voice. 'I tell you, there's going to be trouble.'

'I take it the big man is Ben Adams,' said Denim,

quietly.

'Yes, and he's just killed Joe West, out on the street. Now the whole town is waiting for Two-Gun Pete to arrive.'

Denim smiled at the name. 'Two-Gun Pete – who's he?'

'He's Joe West's brother, and he's deadly with a gun.'

'Where's the sheriff in all this?'

'There's no law here. Two-Gun Pete runs this town.'

Denim was about to ask how the man had been christened with such a silly name, when the saloon doors flung open and a suave-looking man marched in. His white cotton shirt, black leather waistcoat and trousers, and the silver star spurs attached to black patent boots all looked fancy, but most impressive of all were the twin ivory-handled Colts strapped around his waist. He moved fearlessly across the boards and confronted the four men. 'Ben Adams! Which one?' he demanded.

Pulling the long frock coat back to free the gun strapped at his side, the big man stood up. 'I'm Ben Adams,' he snarled. 'Who's asking?'

'You've just killed my brother.'

'He had it coming,' Ben Adams scowled.

Two-Gun Pete's eyes narrowed. 'Say your prayers!'

Chairs kicked away from the table as the other three men stood up to face Two-Gun Pete. Without any warning, Ben Adams pulled his gun; his three friends followed suit. In a blur of movement, the two ivory-handled Colts blazed. Ben Adams slammed into the wall and slid to the floor. His three friends were sent reeling over the chairs. Both guns smoking, Two-

Gun Pete spun around to face Denim. For what seemed a lifetime to Denim, the twin Colts pointed at him. He thought he was about to meet his maker, until the guns twirled on the finger and dropped neatly into their holsters. Without a word, Two-Gun Pete marched out of the saloon. Denim blew a huge sigh of relief. His first encounter with a professional gunslinger was frightening. The speed of action unbelievable.

'You're a lucky fellow,' said the barman. 'When Two-Gun Pete clears leather, it's not often anyone is left alive, especially strangers.' The barman came from behind the counter to inspect the dead men. 'Suppose I'll have to get rid of the bodies.'

'Won't relatives pay for the burial?' asked Denim.

'Nope,' said the barman, as he collected the four men's guns. 'As far as I know, Ben Adams didn't have anyone, and the other three are unknown in these parts,'

'I'll be moving on,' said Denim. 'I need to find work.'

'If you've done any cow punching, then go to the Bar-T ranch,' said the barman. 'There's a big cattle drive starting for Kansas.'

'I've never been on a cattle drive. Where's the Bar-T?'

'A day's ride west. If they set you on, you'll be riding drag.' Not knowing the implications of riding drag, Denim downed his beer and left the barman rooting through the dead men's pockets.

The cattle drive was a new experience for Denim, but he soon learned, to his dismay, that riding drag behind hundreds of longhorns was the dirtiest job he had ever undertaken. Wearing a bandana over his mouth and nose to prevent choking on trail dust, he forced strays back into line. Any mavericks he came across were roped and branded, and ushered back into the herd. The hours were long and the work was backbreaking. After nine long weeks in the saddle and eating tasteless food served up from the chuck wagon, ten thousand beef were driven into corral pens on the outskirts of a large town.

Taking his pay from the trail boss, Denim swore that he would never ride drag again. However, with the first drive behind him he realized there was no better way to see this vast country, so cow punching became his way of life.

Chapter 17

Hell-hole

Riding point most of the time, Denim became known as the best ramrod a trail boss could have. The latest cattle drive took him along the Colorado River, to Eldorado, where hundreds of prospectors hoping to stake their claim in the latest gold rush had erected tents on the outskirts of town.

While the trail boss auctioned the herd to the highest bidder at the pens, Denim explored the town. With two months' pay in his pocket, he found the Pink Lady Saloon and enjoyed washing the trail dust down his throat with beer. It had been more than thirteen years since his escape from the ship, and he had often wondered how his family had fared. Many times he had thought about writing to inform them that he was still alive, but the fear of being traced and captured by the British authorities had always deterred him. As he reminisced, he saw a poster pinned on the side of the bar.

Wanted:

Men to work in the tin mine. Must be strong, fit, and willing. Top rates of pay. Midday prompt! Surveyor's office, next to the bank. First 10 men get the jobs.

Big John (Ganger-man)

The barman noticed Denim's interest. 'Not thinking about working in that death trap, are you?'

'Maybe,' said Denim.

'The townsfolk call it the "Hell-hole".'

'Hell-hole?'

'Someone gets killed there every week.'

'Killed?'

'Explosions. The mine's full of gas pockets, and they haven't got the right equipment to make it safe.'

Denim considered his options. Cattle drives were never-ending and paid just enough money to get by on. Working in the mine sounded dangerous, but if the pay was good, within a short time he would be able to afford a train passage and lodgings in one of the big cities, on the east coast. With jobs aplenty, it would be a better life too. Finishing his beer he went to try his luck.

He was worried about his lack of experience, but when he saw the queue outside the surveyor's office, he realised his fears were unfounded. Skinny young boys, lazy unwashed drunks, and toothless old men had lined up. He surmised that most able bodies were digging for gold in the canyon, or perhaps the death toll at the mine had frightened them away.

Big John appeared in the office doorway. He was visibly disappointed with the turnout, but he signed up six men anyway. The workers were taken by buckboard three miles out of town, to the tin mine. Denim followed on horseback. When they arrived at the mine, Big John gave a roll call. 'Smith and Jones, go to the water tower. Anderson and Jacobs, go to the ore washers. Wilson, you come with me. Armstrong, you join Stone over there by the water chute.' He pointed to a stockily built young man who had a noticeable scar down one side of his face.

Denim followed Stone into the mine. Pulling an ass on a rope, Stone showed the way down a steep gradient with an oil lamp. At the bottom of the shaft, where the tunnel levelled out, he showed Denim how to attach limbers to the ass so it could pull tubs along a narrow-gauge rail track. Going down a long winding tunnel, they eventually came to a candle-lit area where miners, standing on wooden platforms, wielded hammers and pickaxes at the rock walls. Stone and Denim filled the empty tubs with the ore and the ass pulled the load back along the tunnel, and up the steep incline to daylight. Surface workers shoved the tubs to the washers, where the ore was to be graded and cleaned, while Stone and Denim returned with the ass to the bottom of the shaft and waited for the empty tubs.

Minutes later, 'Runaway!' was shouted by one of the surface workers, from the mouth of the mine, and two empty tubs came rolling down the track. As they flew by Stone, he threw a wooden locker into the wheel of each tub and they skidded to a halt at the bottom of the incline. The tubs were hitched to the ass and pulled along the winding tunnel to the miners, to be refilled. This cycle of work was repeated until, ten hours later, a high-pitched siren ended the shift.

'That's your lot, Armstrong,' said Stone. 'First day's over. Take the limbers off the ass and let her go.'

'Won't the ass escape when it gets out of the mine?' asked Denim.

'Don't worry about the ass, Armstrong. It will head straight for the stables.' Denim released the limbers.

'Stand back!' Stone yelled. Bucking like a wild bronco, the ass kicked its rear legs in the air and bolted up the incline.

'Wow! Look at her go,' shrieked Denim, as he watched the animal disappear through the archway of light.

'Yep, she knows where her grub is, all right,' said Stone. 'Now let's go get our food.' They picked up the clothes that they had discarded during the heat of work, and ambled up the incline. Stone put the oil lamp in a toolbox at the entrance of the mine, ready for the next shift, and together they crossed the moonlit yard to the snap cabin. After eating a cooked meal provided by the mining company, they crossed the yard to the bunk shack.

'You can take your pick of beds,' said Stone. 'Six men were killed last week, in an explosion.' Fifteen beds, each separated by a small chest of drawers, filled the long, narrow room. Denim laid on one of the six empty beds and hoped his fate would be different to the last man who slept there. Although Stone was not the most talkative of men, Denim found him to be a good companion.

During the months that followed, Denim hardly ever saw the other men that occupied the bunk shack, for they worked on different shifts. His attention therefore was drawn to the meticulous attention Stone paid to a mustard-coloured waistcoat. Each morning, Stone would take the waistcoat out of the drawer, feel at the contents of a small pocket, and then neatly fold the garment away again. In the evening the same procedure was undertaken before he retired to bed. This ritual was performed daily, and although Denim was curious to know what was so important inside the pocket, he never questioned Stone about it.

With no explosions or deaths in the last eight months, the Hell-hole was not living up to its bad reputation, thought Denim, as he crossed the scrubland to the mine. After drinking and gambling all night in the Pink Lady, he was late for work. He knew that if Big John caught him out, he would lose the job, but without being seen he entered the mine. At the bottom of the shaft he could see a faint light where Stone was hammering rag bolts into the loose tracks.

Denim was halfway down the gradient when he heard the shout: 'Runaway!' An empty tub came flying down the track. He grabbed a wooden locker and threw it at the wheels. The locker hit the spokes and ricocheted into the air.

'Look out!' Denim yelled, as the tub sped down the track.

Stone heard the warning cry and dived out of the way. The tub jumped off the track and crashed into a vertical prop. Part of the roof caved-in and pinned Stone to the rails. 'Runaway!' The shout echoed down the tunnel. Denim grabbed another locker and ran up the gradient to meet the second tub. This time the locker pierced the spokes true. The wheels locked and the tub screeched to a halt at the bottom of the incline, inches away from Stone's face.

Denim ran down the gradient, and pulled Stone free from the rubble. Stone was badly shaken, but with only minor cuts and bruises, he was able to help Denim sprag the roof and clear the fallen debris. Together, they lifted the tubs back onto the track and pushed them down the tunnel. When they came to the ass, which had been frightened by the cave-in, they hitched it to the tubs and carried on working until the siren sounded.

That evening, while sat on their beds in the bunk shack, Stone could see that Armstrong was upset about the incident, so he broke the silence and thanked him for saving his life.

'Goddamn it, Stone,' replied Denim. 'I should have stopped that first tub. I nearly killed you. Late nights, drinking in the Pink Lady have marred my judgement.'

'Don't blame yourself, Armstrong, these things happen. If you hadn't acted as quick as you did, that second tub would have finished me off for sure.' Stone insisted that the matter should rest and with a mutual respect they shook hands, and for the first time since they had met, they talked freely. Eventually, Denim's burning curiosity compelled him to ask about the mustard-coloured waistcoat.

Stone pulled the garment out of the drawer and explained, 'The man who once wore this saved my life.'

'What's in the pocket that you're so frightened of losing?' asked Denim.

Stone laughed at Armstrong's observations and pulled out a silver ring. 'This was my mother's, and this...' he chuckled as he withdrew a reef knot, 'a sailor gave me this, when I was a young boy.'

Denim jumped to his feet. 'Gus! Is your name Gus?'

Stone was amazed that Armstrong knew his first name. By tradition, workers at the mine only ever used surnames. 'Yes, it's Gus, Gus Stone... But, how did you know?'

'Well I'll be,' said Denim. 'You're the boy from the wagon train.'

'Yes, I was on a wagon train with my Ma. But how...?' Stone was too bewildered for words.

'I'm the sailor that gave you the reef knot,' said Denim and, with a big beaming smile, he held out his arms.

Gus was speechless. He jumped up from the bed

and embraced Denim, and like two long-lost brothers they hugged each other in fits of laughter. Gus, who had lost everyone, was joyful at meeting a survivor of the wagon train, while Denim felt he had been reunited with a family member.

'It must be all of thirteen years,' said Denim.

'Fourteen,' corrected Gus. 'But to work together all these months and not recognize one another, it's incredible.'

Exchanging pleasantries on how they had both changed in appearance over the years, Gus sat down on the bed and gave an explicit account of the wagon train massacre. He stroked the tomahawk scar on the side of his face as he remembered. 'Indians killed my Ma and all the homesteaders. Not a soul was left alive. I walked miles without food or water, and if it hadn't been for an old prospector, I would have died. Old Lon found me next to a river, and nursed me back to health. We lived in a log cabin next to an abandoned gold mine, and he reared me like his own son.'

'I was 'bout fifteen when Old Lon came down with yellow fever. I had to go and empty the animal traps in the forest. When I came back the Indians had killed Old Lon, and set fire to the cabin. I buried him by the riverside, but I kept the waistcoat in his remembrance. He was the only father I had ever known. I had nowhere to go, but after travelling some, I got this job at the mine, and I have been here ever since.' Gus put the silver ring and the reef knot back inside the waistcoat pocket and folded it neatly into the drawer. Then he spoke with vengeance. 'I made a vow many years ago, to kill every Indian that I met, and so far I have been true to my word.'

Denim did not doubt him and was quick to say that

he had seen the smoke from the wagons on that fateful day, but he had been too far away to help. Then he told Gus how, as a boy, he had been kidnapped by press gangs, and how Pegs, his best friend, had been killed on the ship before the mutiny and the escape. Finding they had much in common, Denim and Gus bonded like brothers.

Two months later, a gas explosion down the mine caused a fire and killed eight men. Denim was knocked out cold by the blast and would have perished in the flames had it not been for Gus, who risked his own life to save him. The near-death experience unnerved Denim and, feeling lucky to be alive, he decided to get out of the Hell-hole once and for all. He recalled his earlier plans to save money and travel by train to one of the eastern cities, to start a new life, but after twelve months at the gambling tables in the Pink Lady, he had not saved a dime. Perhaps, he thought, he should try his luck at prospecting.

The gold diggers' tents around Eldorado had long since disappeared, but the latest find was up north and, according to the newspapers printed at the telegraph office, gold was so abundant in the Black Hills of Dakota that men were picking nuggets up off the ground. Denim discussed his plans with Gus and, a few weeks later, they upped sticks and left the tin mine for good. Hopeful of striking it rich, they began the long trek up north to join other prospectors in the latest gold rush.

Chapter 18

Showdown in Kirkdeed

Five weeks of riding in the wilderness brought Denim and Gus to Kirkdeed Town, on the outskirts of Wyoming. In need of fresh supplies, they rode down the busy street where people milled around as if a carnival was about to take place. Intrigued by the excitement, they dismounted their horses and mixed with the crowds. Denim nudged the chubby man in front of him. 'What's going on?'

'There's going to be a showdown, over there by the saloon,' said the man. Denim looked in the direction of the Red Drum Saloon, a majestic building two floors high with a brick smokestack built through the apex. Behind a railed balcony, on the first floor, was the biggest drum that he had ever seen. On the street below, townsfolk crowded a tall, slim man who was waving money in his hands. Denim tapped the chubby man again. 'Who's the guy taking bets?'

'You must be strangers around here,' said the man. 'Everyone knows Travis Malone. He owns the saloon, and he's the one that's arranged this showdown.' Annoyed at being pestered, the chubby man moved deeper into the crowd.

As the people parted, Denim caught full sight of the saloon owner. His attire was distinctive: striped grey trousers tucked inside knee-high leather jackboots complemented his tailor-made jacket, while the white shirt, unbuttoned at the top, displayed a royal blue cravat around his neck. A tall black hat, similar to the type seen at notable burial processions in the city, crowned his head. He looked quite the dandy in his flamboyant clothing, but his appearance was marred by his rat-like features: small beady eyes, long pointed nose, and sharp chin. Even though he looked a dubious character, the people were eager to give him their money.

Travis Malone had waited a long time to organize this gambling bonanza. He knew that the sheriff would never allow such a deadly competition to take place, but on learning that the lawman was out of town on a business trip, he took the opportunity to set the plan in motion. After exhausting the collection of bets on the street, he went inside the saloon to his office, and placed the money in the safe. Then he ascended the internal staircase that led to the French doors and the balcony. The man standing beside the big red drum gave it a bang, and the clamour on the street quietened. Travis held his hands high, to make a speech.

'L-a-d-i-e-s and Gen-t-l-e-men, the showdown is about to commence. To enable you to recognize the contestant of your choice: one wears a black hat and the other a white hat. The referee appointed will load each contestant's gun with one bullet, and one bullet only. The two contestants will then proceed to walk from the opposite ends of Main Street and stop at the twenty-pace markers outside the saloon. One bang on the drum will be their signal to draw and fire.' The crowds were jubilant; nothing like this had ever happened in Kirkdeed Town before. 'There can be only one winner,' shouted Travis, 'the surviving contestant will win the prize of two hundred dollars. All winning bets will be paid outside the saloon doors. If both men die, then the contest will be deemed void – no prize money will be awarded and all bets will be refunded.'

More hoorahs sounded as the referee darted on horseback from one end of Main Street to the other. Loading each contestant's gun with one bullet, the referee rode back to the saloon to watch the showdown from the vantage point of the horse's back.

Travis knew that the build-up to a showdown was all important. If he kept the crowd captivated and they enjoyed the thrill, they would come back another time and gamble more money. Waving a red bandana, he signalled the contestants to start their walk. People buzzed with excitement and shouted encouragement to the gunman that they had gambled on.

Reaching the twenty-pace markers, the contestants stopped to face each other. Hands hovering over their guns, they waited for the bang of the drum. Denim analysed the two gunmen: the man wearing the white hat looked young and nervous, but the older man wearing the black hat appeared calm and collected and every bit the winner. From the rooftop of the saloon a reflection of sunlight caught Denim's eye. A man was hiding behind the chimney stack, aiming a rifle.

Suddenly, there was an uproar among the crowds as the sheriff bustled his way to the front. 'Stop the fight! Stop the fight!' he shouted. Angered by the unexpected arrival of the lawman, Travis signalled to the drummer. At the sound of the drum the two gunmen drew and fired. In that same instant, a rifle shot sent the contestant's white hat sailing into the air. Gunfire from Denim, brought the rifleman rolling down the roof.

When Travis saw the rifleman thud onto the street, he knew that his ingenious plan had failed. He had tricked the townsfolk into gambling on the gunman wearing the white hat, by offering greater betting odds. Then he had colluded with the referee to put blank bullets into each contestant's gun, so that neither man could kill the other. The rifleman on the rooftop had been paid to shoot dead the gunman wearing the white hat. Three gunshots would have sounded like one and it would have appeared to the crowds that the contestant wearing the black hat had killed his opponent. All Travis had to do was dispose of the dead body before anyone realized a rifle shot had been the killer and, after paying out the prize money, most of the takings would have been his. But this sharpshooting stranger and the sheriff had ruined everything. Travis knew that when the townsfolk found out that he had duped them, they would want to lynch him. He had to escape, but first he would take all the money from the safe.

Realizing the showdown had been rigged against him, the young contestant saw Travis running across the balcony. Quickly, he reloaded the gun from his cartridge belt and aimed.

'I'll have that,' said the sheriff, snatching the weapon out of the young man's hand.

'Hold it!' said Gus, as he prodded the barrel of his gun into the lawman's back. He threw the sheriff's firearm into a water trough, and then lobbed the other gun back to its owner. The young man caught it, aimed, and fired. Travis had disappeared through the French doors, but the drummer, crashed over the balcony with a bullet between the eyes.

The saloon doors burst wide open. Travis came bounding into the street. Holding a moneybag in each hand, he ran to his horse. Two shots from the young man sent Travis sprawling across the ground. The money bags split open. Coins rolled along the floor.

Paper money flew high on the wind. Tumbling over one another, the townsfolk scrambled to catch the flying dollars.

Seeing the fate of Travis, the referee kicked the horse into flight and tried to escape. A shot from the young man blasted the referee out of the saddle. As he fell, his foot caught in the stirrup. At a gallop the frightened horse dragged him down the street.

Jumping onto their mounts, Denim and Gus spurred them into action and galloped out of town. The young man leapt onto the nearest horse and followed. Turning in the saddle he fired one last shot. The contestant wearing the black hat sagged onto his knees. For a few seconds he remained in that position, then he slumped face down into the dirt. The black hat rolled away on the wind.

Eastern newspapers dubbed the three fugitives the 'Kirkdeed Trio', and the County Law Enforcement Office dispatched dead or alive posters to all neighbouring towns. Forced into a life of crime, the trio attempted to hold up wagons that carried miners' wages, but the sharpshooters riding vanguard were too vigilant.

After a failed bank robbery and being hunted by a posse for days on end, they withdrew to a hideout in the hillsides to rethink their plans. While sitting around a campfire, Denim and Gus learned that their new-found friend was none other than Kid Rio, the boy killer from Rialto Town. Gus told how he had once seen a wanted poster of the boy when visiting a town with Old Lon. Denim recounted the night, when a young boy on horseback nearly trampled him to death at Rialto Springs Waterfall. Kid Rio confessed that he was the boy rider, and apologized.

Denim acknowledged with a nod of the head and then asked, 'Back in Kirkdeed Town, I noticed that you used the cavalry-twist to draw your gun. How come?'

Kid Rio had no idea that his draw had a name, but he endeavoured to explain. 'I once came across an abandoned army fort. Inside the barracks I found this cavalry holster. I cut off the fastening flap, but the gun would only fit in one way, with the handle facing forward. I tried different ways of drawing, but the cavalry-twist, as you put it, was the easiest for me.'

'You're pretty slick with that shooter,' said Denim. 'Somebody teach you?'

'Comes natural, I guess.' Kid Rio did not want them to know about the strange powers that the gun possessed.

'You're the fastest I've ever seen with a gun,' said Gus.

'Nope, there's another,' said Denim, 'and he's even faster.' He remembered vividly the shootout in Jackson Town, and how easily Two-Gun Pete had killed four men, but he gave no detail. Kid Rio did not like the idea that someone was faster, but he let the remark go. He had a lot to thank these two men for; they had saved his life, but they did not know what he knew about the gun.

'Tell us, what did happen in Rialto Town all those years ago?' asked Denim.

Kid Rio gave a harrowing account of his life: how his family had been driven out of every town they had entered, just because they were Mormons; how his evil father had made life a misery for him; about the bounty hunter who had terrified the town and killed two men before giving him the gun; and about the day of reckoning, when he killed the schoolboy, the teacher, and his own father, and escaped from the Mormon camp. Kid Rio pulled the shiny black revolver from its holster. 'And it was with this gun that I gained my revenge.'

After listening to Kid Rio's story, Denim was not surprised that the boy had turned man-killer, but Gus was only interested in the gun. 'Let's have a look,' said Gus, holding out his hand.

'No!' Kid Rio dropped the gun sharply into its holster. The rebuff made Gus angry. He jumped to his feet. Kid Rio reared up to face him. A dangerous silence prevailed between the two men until Denim shot a keen glance at Kid Rio. Not wanting to lose their friendship, Kid Rio backed off and apologized. 'Sorry for being so surly, Gus, but the gun has been a life changer for me, as I have already explained, and I don't let anyone touch it.'

Mellowing with the explanation, Gus settled by the fire. The warmth of the flames made him feel secure, just as they had when he was a boy on the wagon train, and he was soon nodding. Too easy to get shot in the firelight, Kid Rio always said, and moved into the shadows.

While his two friends slept, Denim stoked the campfire with sagebrush, and mulled over their options. Obtaining honest jobs was out of the question due to the reward money hanging over their heads, and holding up stagecoaches would only offer slim pickings. Robbing trains was too dangerous – sometimes soldiers were deployed to track down the offenders. After much thought without any conclusions, he was about to give up on getting any new ideas, when Travis Malone came to mind. Showdowns – that's it, thought Denim; that is the answer. He had always been impressed with Kid

Rio's shooting skills; not many men would beat him to the draw. Satisfied that he had found a solution to their problems, he rested his back against a tree and slept.

While drinking coffee around a rekindled fire the next morning, he told his two friends about his plan. Gus shook his head in doubt. 'How can we entice any challengers for a showdown, without money? We're skint.'

'We'll use the gamblers' bets as the prize money,' said Denim. 'All we have to do is find a fast gun that has a reputation, and we all know that there's one in every town, and most of the locals would bet on him winning.'

Gus shook his head in disagreement. 'No one would be interested. Kid Rio's not a known gunfighter. What happened all those years ago, when he was a boy, has long since been forgotten.'

'When Kid Rio's name spreads throughout the counties, there will be queues of gunfighters wanting to take him on,' said Denim convincingly, 'and not just for the prize money, but to prove that they are faster.' Kid Rio liked the sound of it. While he had possession of the shiny black gun he knew he could not lose.

'We'll offer a hundred dollars for the first showdown,' said Denim, enthusiastically.

'What if Kid Rio loses?' said Gus. Kid Rio flashed a stark look at Gus; he was not happy with that remark.

'Come on, Gus,' urged Denim. 'You said yourself – Kid Rio's the fastest gun you ever saw. We'll start in the small towns first, and when Kid Rio's name is on everybody's lips, we'll move to larger towns. In no time at all we'll have enough money to buy a spread of our own, and retire to the country.'

Gus was not sure. 'What's going to stop the law from hunting us down?'

'All we have to do is keep to the towns out west,' answered Denim. 'Most of the lawmen out there are corrupt and can be bought. And by the time a showdown has been arranged, it will be over and we'll be long gone with the money.' He lifted his eyebrows to emphasize the point.

By now, Gus and Kid Rio were both nodding their heads in agreement and – just like all those years ago, when Denim became leader of the boys playing pirates in Portsmouth Docks – he had taken full control of the Kirkdeed Trio.

Chapter 19

The Black Hill Gang

After a number of face-offs in small towns, the showdowns became a success. The infamous name of the boy killer was resurrected, and Kid Rio became known as one of the deadliest of gunfighters. Tales of his expertise with a gun and his merciless killings spread quickly, far and wide, and people became frightened at the mere mention of his name.

News of the showdowns came to the attention of cattle barons in Kansas and, always eager to make more money, they sent a go-between to meet the trio with a proposition. In return for arranging showdowns in major towns and increasing the prize money to $300, they would take all the gambling bets on the street.

As the showdowns exploited the larger towns, the deal became financially rewarding for both sides, but always at the expense of another gunfighter, for Kid Rio always shot to kill. After six months, and eleven dead men, it was proving difficult to find a new contender until Kid Rio suggested taking on two opponents at the same time. Denim and Gus thought he was *loco* and tried to talk him out of it, but the cattle barons were thrilled with the idea and increased the prize money to $800. This created new interest, and people came in droves to Abilene Town in Kansas, to see if Kid Rio could win against two opponents.

Sheriff Jackson, who had been bribed to allow the gunfight in his town, made his way across the busy streets of Abilene to the Red House Hotel. Inside the restaurant, he found Denim sat next to a tall grandfather clock. He pulled up a chair and introduced himself with the news that Tom and Wes Clancy were the opponents for the next day's fight.

Realizing the sheriff was adding importance to the men's names, Denim asked, 'Who are they?'

'They're the leaders of the Black Hill Gang, and if the rest of them should show up, it might be wise to call the showdown off.'

'If any more of the gang come into town let me know,' said Denim, 'I'd appreciate it.'

'OK' said the sheriff, pushing away from the table. 'Showdown's noon tomorrow, opposite the clock tower in the town square.' That said, he left the restaurant.

Upstairs in the hotel, Denim informed his two friends. Gus had heard of the Black Hill Gang's notoriety, and he was in favour of getting out of town while the going was good. Kid Rio was not ruffled and explained, 'If I do not show up, the people will say that I had shied scared. They would lose interest in the showdowns, and the cattle barons would not sponsor the fights anymore.' Denim knew Kid Rio was right, so he let the matter drop; showdowns were their meal ticket.

That evening in the bustling bar room of the White Eagle Saloon, the sheriff made Denim aware that five more of the Black Hill Gang had arrived. He pointed them out – sat at the gaming tables with the Clancy brothers. Wes Clancy happened to spot the sheriff looking over and, recognizing Kid Rio from a wanted poster, he sauntered over to the bar. His brother followed.

'Well... If it isn't the kid killer himself,' slurred

Wes Clancy.

Kid Rio's hand dropped to his gun. The crowded room hushed to a silence. Quickly, Denim stepped between the two men. Tom Clancy pulled on his younger brother's arm. 'Leave it, Wes. Leave it till tomorrow.' Pushing by the two brothers, Denim and Gus steered Kid Rio towards the exit.

'Well, look at that,' shouted Wes Clancy to the crowd watching. 'The boy killer's gone and got a nursemaid.' Guffaws of laughter filled the room.

Kid Rio turned to go back, but Denim and Gus blocked his way. 'Don't be a fool,' said Denim, as he squeezed Kid Rio out of the doors. 'If you kill him now, we'll lose our biggest payout.' Kid Rio was livid. He could not wait for tomorrow.

Next day, people came into town in wagon loads from the surrounding areas. Four moderators, chosen by the sheriff, mingled with the visitors on the street and collected wagers. All betting stopped before midday and the stakes were locked in the jailhouse safe. Sheriff Jackson picked up his carbine rifle and, along with the deputy, he walked through the overcrowded streets to the Red House Hotel. Finding the trio sat in the restaurant, he broke the latest news. 'Wes Clancy had one drink too many last night. He was bragging to the barman that they intend to kill you three for the bounty money, and then take the prize money and all the gambling bets.'

'Have any more of the gang showed up?' asked Denim.

'According to the barman, there's at least eleven men backing the brothers.'

'That's thirteen against three then,' said Denim.

'Nope,' said Sheriff Jackson. 'It's thirteen against

five. If they are going to take the gambling money, the gang have got to rob the jailhouse safe and that involves me and my deputy. We stand a far better chance of stopping them if we throw in with you now.'

'Good! They won't be expecting five of us,' said Denim. He looked at the tall grandfather clock. It was almost time. 'Let's go.'

Denim and Gus weaved their way through the crowded sidewalks and took up positions on the corner of the square. On the other side of the street, Sheriff Jackson and his deputy faced the clock tower. Making his way down the centre of the street, Kid Rio touched the handle of his gun for reassurance. He felt the warm tingling sensations. The power was there. A faint smile creased his lips as he entered the middle of the square and stopped fifteen paces short of the two brothers.

Tom Clancy was brimming with confidence; he knew he could not lose. His gang was hiding all around. Wes Clancy was a worried man. Although he had shot and killed several men before, he had never faced a man in a shootout. All those stories he had heard about Kid Rio's speed with a gun played on his mind. Could they be true? He glanced at the tower clock: five minutes before noon. Sweat trickled down the nape of his neck. His breathing became shallow. His heart thumped against his chest. He could not wait any longer – he drew his gun.

The gang opened fire. Bullets exploded in all directions. Townsfolk ran for cover. Caught in the crossfire, bodies dropped in the street. Rifle shots from the clock tower felled the deputy. Blood pouring from his leg, he crawled to a doorway. A round of bullets from the sheriff's carbine brought that rifleman tumbling from the tower. Rapid gunshots from a supply wagon made the sheriff run for cover. Denim fired at the team of horses harnessed to the wagon. The horses panicked and bolted across the square. Two men jumped out of the wagon and ran towards the clock tower. Successive shots from the deputy sent one runner crashing through a shop window, and the second man reeling into a water trough. From an upstairs window, two of the gang plunged headlong onto the street as Denim proved his accuracy with a gun. Five men dashed out of a large building, guns blazing they raced to their horses. Gus downed two, but return fire winged him in the arm. As the men mounted their steeds Denim ran into the middle of the square shooting. One rider rode hard at Denim, trying to mow him down. A volley of shots from Denim blasted that man out of the saddle. The last two riders tried to escape the slaughter by galloping out of town. One was picked off by the sheriff's carbine, but the other man lived to tell the tale.

As the shooting stopped everyone looked over and saw Wes Clancy facing Kid Rio. Wes had drawn his gun first, but when he saw his brother shot dead by Kid Rio, he had frozen. Unable to pull the trigger he had watched his brother die, and now Kid Rio's gun was pointing at him. He could see the dead gang members strewn about the square and he knew he was next. Then he had a glimmer of hope. He saw a rifle on the rooftops aimed at Kid Rio's back. In a speed that beguiled Wes Clancy, Kid Rio turned and fired and the last bushwhacker fell to his death. Then the shiny black gun was pointing at Wes Clancy and he knew, now, that all the stories he had ever heard about Kid Rio's skill with a gun were true.

'Who needs a nursemaid now?' snarled Kid Rio. There was a moment of silence as both men, gun in hand, faced one another. Suddenly, Kid Rio spun the shiny black gun into its holster. His cruel lips smirked, 'Make your move, Clancy.'

Wes Clancy could not believe the chance he was being given. All he had to do was lift the gun in his hand and pull the trigger. Surely he could do that before Kid Rio had time to draw again. No one could be that fast! Could they? He began to doubt himself. Death was beckoning. The tower clock clanged noon. Quickly, he lifted the gun. Blood splattered his face. Burning fire ripped through his chest. Full length, he hit the dirt. Fifteen paces away stood the harbinger of death. Kid Rio slid the shiny black gun back inside its holster.

Townsfolk ran to aid the civilians who had been caught in the crossfire. Sheriff Jackson shouted for a doctor, and then helped the wounded deputy back to the jailhouse. In need of medical attention, Gus followed, while Denim and Kid Rio dragged the dead gang members into the middle of the square.

'That's the last one,' shouted Kid Rio, as he lined the bodies up.

'Twelve in all,' said Denim.

'Yep, pity the thirteenth got away.'

'Lucky for some,' smiled Denim. He knew that Kid Rio would have killed them all. 'Let's go and see how Gus is making out.'

When they arrived at the sheriff's office, the town doctor was in the process of removing the bullet from the deputy's leg, but Gus was bandaged and ready to travel. Sheriff Jackson opened the safe, and handed $800 prize money to Denim.

'No doubt the go-between will sort out the cattle

barons' debt,' said the sheriff.

'No doubt,' said Denim. 'But we're moving on. The Black Hill Gang should fetch a tidy sum in bounty money though. You're welcome to it.'

'Much obliged,' said sheriff Jackson, 'I'll share it with the deputy.'

'*Adios*,' said Denim. The Kirkdeed Trio rode out of town, leaving the streets of Abilene littered with dead.

Chapter 20

The Last Showdown

News of the Abilene Town bloodbath spread far and wide. When the media in the eastern cities reported that civilians were being killed in showdowns, there was a public outcry that demanded the men responsible for such atrocities should be brought to justice. Ultimately, the Allan Pinkerton Agency was commissioned by the authorities to hunt down the Kirkdeed Trio and bring them in, dead or alive.

Fearing criminal proceedings, the cattle barons decided on one last showdown. They had lost a lot of money by backing the Clancy brothers to win, and they wanted to recoup their losses. Knowing the public would gamble even more money on Kid Rio, especially now that he had beaten two opponents together, and in the hope of attracting a professional gunslinger that could beat him, they increased the prize money to $2,000. Determined to go out on a high, the cattle barons instructed the go-between to search farther west, for a lawman that would be willing to stage the last showdown. Sheriff John Brassica, of Cripple Creek, Utah, was one such man.

Three weeks after wiping out the Black Hill Gang, the Kirkdeed Trio crossed the Colorado River and rode into Cripple Creek Town. They were amazed at their reception. Welcome banners flew high from one building to the next. Crowds cheered in a carnival atmosphere as a band paraded up and down the streets. Sherriff John Brassica greeted the three men and escorted them to Grand Hotel, where Julie, the attractive middle-aged proprietor, showed them their rooms. 'All at the expense of the cattle barons,' she said. 'You must be special?'

Travel weary and saddle sore, the trio retired to their rooms. Denim had almost fallen asleep when an errand boy knocked on the door and handed him a written message.

Diamond Jacks Casino.
John Starett

Denim gave the boy a tip and then got ready. He had met the cattle barons' go-between twice before, and he did not like the man. Following Julie's directions, he found John Starett sitting in a quiet lounge of the casino. Denim pulled up a chair and poured himself a measure of whiskey from the bottle on the table. 'Whereabouts is the showdown going to take place?' he asked.

'The sheriff will give you those details tomorrow,' said John Starett. 'Meanwhile, I must warn you that the Pinkertons have been commissioned to track the Kirkdeed Trio down and, because of this unfortunate situation, this will be the last showdown sponsored by the cattle barons.'

'So they're pulling out?' Denim had wondered why the prize money had been increased so dramatically.

'The cattle barons can't afford their good names to be associated with the deaths of civilians. There's been a huge outcry in the city.'

The excuse made sense to Denim. 'Has the other gunfighter arrived yet?'

'Yes, but I've arranged his accommodation at the other end of town, so that the two competitors do not meet until the day of the showdown. After what happened in the White Eagle Saloon with the Clancy brothers, I thought it best.'

'What part of the country is he from?' asked Denim.

'Missouri, I believe.'

Denim pondered a moment. 'What's his line, and why is he willing to risk his neck?'

'I understand that he was running for the mayor's office in his local town, but when several notable citizens, who were his rivals, suddenly died, the Texas Rangers descended. They arrested all those involved, but he managed to escape. Apparently, two thousand dollars prize money is the stake he needs to get him started again.'

'Has he got a reputation with a gun?' asked Denim.

'Evidently, but he's not well known around these parts.'

The slightest grin on John Starett's face irritated Denim. He did not trust the man. 'What's the gunfighter's name?'

John Starett took his time refilling his whiskey glass and then he took a long, slow sip. Denim's angry stare demanded an answer. 'Oh, I'm sorry,' said John Starett, 'what was the question?'

Annoyed with the man's guile, Denim's voice deepened. 'The name!'

'Ah, yes, his name. It's Pete... Pete West.'

A cold shiver ran down Denim's spine. He pictured twin ivory-handled Colts springing into action to blast four men to instant death. Many years had passed since Jackson Town, but the memory of Two-Gun Pete was as vivid as yesterday. Denim shoved away from the table.

'Oh, is it something I have said?' John Starett quipped.

'I'll see you tomorrow,' said Denim. 'Have the prize money ready.'

'Goodnight,' shouted John Starett. A cunning smile flitted across his face. This time, Kid Rio had a real fight on his hands.

Denim made haste back to the hotel. In Kid Rio's room, he told his two friends the news. 'Remember I once told you that there was another gunman, and he was even faster than Kid Rio? Well that man is here in town, and he's the opponent for tomorrow's showdown.' Denim waited for some response, but his two friends made no comment, so he recounted the day that Two-Gun Pete killed the four gunmen.

'If he's that good,' said Gus, 'then we should leave town, tonight.'

'That's right,' said Denim. 'The prize money isn't worth getting killed for.'

Kid Rio scoffed at his two friends' alarm. 'Two-Gun Pete? Huh, it's a joke!' He remembered what the bounty hunter had told him: *If you're good enough, you only need one gun.*

'It's no joke,' raged Denim. 'This man's exceptional with a gun.'

'Don't worry Denim, I'll beat him just like I did all the others,' Kid Rio bragged.

'The others were just two-bit local bums in comparison to this gunfighter,' stressed Denim.

'What about the Clancy brothers?' said Kid Rio. 'They were more than that.'

'I agree,' said Denim, 'but this man is a professional killer. He's been around for a long time, and no one has managed to lower his colours yet. If you take him on, then you're a dead man.'

Kid Rio lay back on his bed and closed his eyes. All he knew was that, while he had possession of the gun, he was unbeatable. Its strange power had saved him many times and, no matter how strong the danger, it had always managed to lift his game play to the next level. Kid Rio was confident. Since the Clancy shoot-out, Denim had seen Kid Rio's ego grow bigger than his stature, and he knew there would be no talking him out of it. He tapped Gus on the arm, and together they left the room.

The next morning, Denim was awakened by the activity outside the hotel. He pulled the curtains back and looked out of the bedroom window. The streets were bustling. Wagons were rolling in by the dozen. Children played with stringed balloons and ate candy as if at a carnival. Already, the touts were taking bets. Denim dressed and strapped on his gun. Downstairs, he joined Gus and Rio in the restaurant for a late breakfast. Not a word was spoken between the three men; each had his own ideas about the oncoming fight.

Deep in thought, Denim realized he was staring at Julie, who was busy arranging small vases of flowers on white cloth dining tables. Her attractiveness stirred his emotions. He questioned why, after all these years, he had not taken a partner and settled down. Instead, he had become embroiled in showdowns and moving from county to county to avoid the law – and right now, there was a question mark hanging over that way of life. If Kid Rio was killed, he wondered what he and Gus would do. Thanking Julie for her hospitality, the trio left the hotel. Outside, Sheriff John Brassica appeared with information that Two-Gun Pete was waiting outside the Gospel Centre.

Kid Rio spun the bullet chamber of the gun. It was fully loaded. A warm tingling glow surged through his body. He was ready. As he made his way down the centre of the street, people on the crowded sidewalks hoorayed and shouted their support. On reaching the Gospel Centre, he found that Two-Gun Pete was not there. He shielded his eyes from the sun and looked to the far end of the street. A silhouetted figure was advancing. Twin Colts flashed sunlight with every step. At a dozen paces, Two-Gun Pete stopped to face Kid Rio.

A weird sense overcame Denim as he watched from the sidewalk. Seeing Two-Gun Pete again, after all those years, felt strange. The man had not aged and his attire was as striking as ever: a brown vaquero jacket with contrasting black embroidered lapels and cuffs that matched the handstitched sugar loaf hat. A black string tie pinched the collar of his white frilled shirt, which was neatly tucked into the red sash around his waist. Sparkling concho buttons hemmed the leggings of dark brown, flared trousers, which stopped short of the silver star spurs attached to his leather boots. But, most stunning of all, were the two ivory-handled guns housed in silver-studded black holsters. He looked immaculate – and invincible. Denim wished now that he had done more to convince Kid Rio to leave town.

An extreme silence descended upon the watching crowds. Frightened children, sensing something macabre was about to happen, ran to their parents. For what seemed an eternity the two gunmen stood straight-legged, staring at one another. There were no nervous trigger fingers here. And no sweating brows. Each looked for a weakness in the other. That brief second when one might blink, or sigh a breath. Then, as if synchronized, the two men crouched into the gunfighter's stance. With blinding speed they drew their guns. Three shots exploded as one. Wisps of gun smoke blew away on the wind. The crowds gasped in astonishment to see both men, guns drawn, still standing. Neither man moved. Then Kid Rio's gun hand dropped loosely by his side. His gun pointed to the ground. Denim feared the worst.

A broad grin creased Two-Gun Pete's face. He spun the two ivory-handled guns on the finger and dropped them expertly back into their holsters. Suddenly, his smile faded. He clutched at his chest as blood oozed through the fancy white shirt. Face contorted in disbelief, he crumpled to the ground. In bravado, Kid Rio lifted the shiny black gun to his lips and blew the smoke away from the barrel. The town came alive. Most of them had gambled on Kid Rio to win. Crowds danced and cheered loudly while the band boomed out a raucous celebration tune.

Denim was relieved that Kid Rio had won, but as he looked at Two-Gun Pete lying in the dirt, he felt a touch of remorse. The death of such a colourful character was saddening. The man had been a living legend. Then he looked at the crowds rejoicing at the man's death and, just like all those years ago when he had watched the first hanging on the ship, he was repulsed by their behaviour.

Sheriff John Brassica was first on the scene. He claimed the two ivory-handled guns for his own. Then he showed Denim the telegram he had received, just before the showdown.

Pinkertons on their way to Cripple Creek.
Sherriff, Hudson.
Shylock Town. 11:55 am

'How long before they get here?' asked Denim.

'About an hour's ride,' said the sheriff.

'Where's the prize money?'

'Starett's got it.'

'What about the gambling money?'

'He's got that too,' said the sheriff, 'but most of it needs to be paid out to the people. The cattle barons took a huge loss; they gambled on Two-Gun Pete winning.'

Moving quickly down the street, Denim realized that the cattle barons and John Starett had planned on Kid Rio being killed. He drew his gun in anger. Charging through the casino doors he found John Starett, bags packed, ready to leave town.

'Now hold on, Denim,' said Starett, holding both hands in the air. 'I've done nothing wrong.'

'Where's the prize money?'

'In the bag, over there. I was just bringing it to you.'

'I bet you were!' Denim picked up the bag, and dead-eyed Starett. 'Two grand?'

'Yes! Yes! It's all there, I promise.' Denim pointed the gun at Starett's head. The go-between dropped to his knees and begged for his life. Denim eased the trigger. Satisfied in the knowledge that the cattle barons had taken another huge loss, he left John Starett alive, but a broken man, weeping on the casino floor.

Chapter 21

A Town Called No Name

In an attempt to shake the Pinkertons off their trail, the Kirkdeed Trio travelled through the red rocks of Utah, and then south across the mud flats of Arizona. They rode fast, for days and then weeks, but the Pinkertons still followed. As the monotonous, grey skies shortened, and the nights became colder, they found a cave big enough to stable their horses, and then they set about stockpiling brushwood from the surrounding thickets. Within days, bitter winds had dropped the temperature below freezing. Trees disappeared from view, as rocky hillsides were transformed into castles of snow. Unable to leave the cave for weeks, they boiled ice for water, and roasted small rodents that they caught for food. On days when the snow eased they were lucky to bag a quail, or a ptarmigan; however, even with so little nourishment, they managed to survive the bleak winter months.

When the big thaw came, Denim hoped the law had given up the chase, but he was not banking on it. The Pinkertons were renowned for getting their man, and he knew it would not be long before they were forced into a shootout with them. If they could get to Mexico, he knew they would be safe. Not many law officers ever crossed the border; it was out of their jurisdiction. With overgrown hair, curly moustaches, and pointed beards, the gaunt, dishevelled trio got back on the trail.

Daylight was fast fading when they came to a signboard. *No Name Town* had been scorched into the wood. 'No name, eh?' Kid Rio spat at the board.

'We'll see.'

The outskirts of the town looked bleak as howling winds whipped up a sandstorm. They covered their faces with bandanas and pulled their hats down low. As they rode down deserted streets, balls of tumbleweed rolled on the wind. Sand drifted high against abandoned, white-washed, adobe buildings. Loose doors and windows banged open and close, while metal smokestacks clanked on rooftops. Looks like a ghost town, thought Denim, until he spotted a faint light coming from Pedro's Cantina.

Securing their horses to a post, the trio held on to their hats and ran inside. A plump Mexican man was slouched behind a dingily lit counter, listening to four old men having a loud debate. Sat at the only table in the room, the four old-timers were so engrossed in argument that they did not notice the three strangers' arrival.

'Whiskey,' ordered Denim.

The Mexican shoved a bottle and three glasses across the counter, then he lumbered back to the other end of the bar and carried on listening to the debate. 'Yes siree,' said the first old-timer, puffing heavily on a long straw pipe. 'Everybody's talking about the Kid. They say he's meaner than Sam Bass, and faster on the draw than Johnny Ringo.'

The second old-timer spat a streaky volume of brown tobacco juice into a spittoon at the foot of the bar. 'I don't know about that,' he said, 'the Kid would have to be mighty fast to beat Ringo.'

'Huh,' scoffed the pipe-smoker, 'Ringo would have nothing to come against the Kid. Why, they reckon the Kid would even outdraw Wes Hardin, never mind about Johnny Ringo.'

'It's true,' shouted Pedro from the bar. 'They say

the Kid is the Fastest Gun Alive, and no one can beat him.'

The pipe-smoker lifted the hearing horn hung around his neck and put it to his ear. 'Eh! What did you say?'

Pedro repeated, a little louder, 'They say the Kid is the Fastest Gun Alive and no one can beat him.'

'That's right,' said the pipe-smoker, lowering the horn. 'That's what everyone's saying all right. And I'll tell you this: the Kid has killed many a man who dared to say otherwise.'

Denim was amused. If only the old-timers knew that they were in the Kid's company right now. He looked at Gus, and nodded in the direction of Kid Rio, who was standing tall in recognition that the old-timers were talking about him.

In a shower of spit, a toothless old-timer joined the argument. 'I heard that this new gunslinger is even faster than Kid Rio.'

The fourth old-timer banged his whittling stick on the floorboards for attention. 'What? Faster than Kid Rio. Well I'll be hornswoggled.'

Denim was surprised; the old-timers were not talking about Kid Rio after all. He shot a quick glance at his friend, who was gritting his teeth.

From the bar, Pedro interrupted again, 'I was in Dodge City, when the marshal called the new gunslinger out on the street. The lawman didn't even clear leather afore the Kid shot him dead.'

The whittling stick rattled loudly. 'That's nothing,' said the old-timer. 'Kid Rio once killed three gunfighters all at the same time, and not one of them managed to draw their gun.'

'Haw, that takes some believing,' scoffed the tobacco-chewer, juice dribbling down his chin.

'Cheyenne Town is where it happened,' said the old man with the whittling stick, as he tried to convince the others. 'And I can tell you this, Kid Rio was *m-i-g-h-t-y* fast. The fastest I've ever seen.'

'Why, I heard tell that Kid Rio was dead,' said the pipe-smoker, 'so he couldn't have been that fast.' He chuckled merrily at having ridiculed the other man's story.

'Kid Rio dead?' said the toothless old-timer, as he licked his lips and drew in the slaver. 'I don't believe it. Who shot him, then?'

'Wild Bill Hickok gunned him down last summer, in Tucson,' said the pipe-smoker. 'They say Kid Rio didn't stand a chance against Wild Bill.' The pipe-smoker took a long swig of beer. This seemed to be the signal for the rest of the table to do the same.

Denim could see that Kid Rio was getting angry. So, before his friend could do anything rash, he decided to intervene. 'Hey, old men!' Surprised by the shout, the four old-timers turned and, for the first time, they saw the three unkempt strangers standing at the bar. 'Have any of you ever seen Wes Hardin, or Wild Bill Hickok, or Kid Rio for that matter?' asked Denim.

A short silence prevailed until the pipe-smoker answered, 'No! But we sure as hell would know them if any of them happened to come in here!' He guffawed loudly as he looked at his companions to see if they had enjoyed his joke. The tobacco-chewer slapped his thigh and hooted with laughter. Sniggering breathlessly, the toothless old-timer showered the table with spit, while the old-timer with the whittling stick chortled loudest of all.

Kid Rio straightened up from the bar. His hand dropped menacingly to the handle of his gun. The laughter stopped. 'Who is this Fastest Gun Alive?' Kid Rio demanded. 'And where do I find him?'

The pipe-smoker took it on himself to answer. 'Hang Tree Falls is where you'll find him. And Billy the Kid is the name.'

Kid Rio turned to Pedro. 'Hang Tree Falls – which way?'

'Sixty miles south, *amigo*. Near the Mexican border.'

Glancing at his two friends, Kid Rio nodded towards the door. 'Hang Tree Falls,' he said. All three downed their whiskeys and headed for the street.

'Hey! *Gringos*,' a demanding voice shouted from the bar. The trio turned as one and stared at the Mexican. Instantly, Pedro realized that the strangers were more dangerous than their untidy appearance portrayed. He shrugged his shoulders in a subservient gesture and held his hands out. 'Er, no offence *amigos*, but you forgot to pay for your drinks.'

Denim tossed two dollar coins into the air, towards the bar. The shiny black gun flew into Kid Rio's hand. Two blasts bounced the coins off the wall and sent them spinning onto the table. As they came to rest, the four old-timers gasped in amazement. Each coin had a bullet hole plumb centre. Kid Rio glared menacingly at Pedro. For a few seconds he thought about killing the man. Then, he let the gun drop into its holster and joined his two friends outside the cantina.

Pedro blew a huge sigh of relief. He knew he had been close to death. A loud argument erupted as the four old-timers tried to guess who the sharpshooter was. And if Kid Rio had happened to return years later to No Name Town, he would have been outraged to find in Pedro's Cantina two silver dollars, with holes pierced dead centre, mounted in a glass case on the wall. Inscribed on a brass plaque were the words:

Both coins were shot simultaneously,
while in mid-air,
by Wild Bill Hickok
April 14th, 1875

Chapter 22

Old Enemies and Old Friends

Two days' riding brought the trio to the Mexican border where a huge granite boulder divided the trail. Directions had been scored onto the rock:

Hang Tree Falls – 10 miles – East
Boston Wharf – 15 miles – South

Denim read the name 'Boston Wharf' and became transfixed. Long-forgotten memories stirred. He touched the locket hanging around his neck and was overcome by a sense of inevitability, as if he was fated to be here. He remembered Pegs' letter that he had found in the trinket box on the ship:

If you should ever be in the south of the Americas and you happen to come across Boston Wharf, my dying wish would be for you to visit Rosie's Cantina and seek out Katie. Give her the locket and explain why I never returned – but, most of all, let her know of my undying love.

'What's up?' queried Kid Rio.
Coming out of the trance, Denim replied, 'Oh, nothing. I'm just plumb tuckered out, I guess.' But his obligation to Pegs was uppermost in his mind when he said, 'There's a river up yonder, we'll make camp there.' He needed time to think things out.
There had been little rain since the winter snows and the land here had become arid, severely narrowing the river. Even so, the remaining trickle

was enough to scrub up and water the horses. After shaving and cutting their overgrown hair, the trio managed to shoot a white-tailed deer that had come down to the river. As they sat around the campfire feasting on venison, Denim decided to tell his two friends that he would be riding to Boston Wharf at daybreak, in his quest to find Katie. Both men argued that they should go with him, in case the military officials at the port recognized him. But when Denim explained that this was something that he must do alone, in memory of Pegs, they relented and agreed to wait by the river for his return.

While his two friends slept, Denim sat with his back against a tree and opened the locket to look at the portrait. No wonder Pegs had been captivated by Katie's charm; she was beautiful. After all these years, he wondered how she would receive the news of Pegs' death. He put the locket around his neck and thought how strange were the destinies of life. For fifteen years he had avoided going near any port, for fear of being recognized and captured, but now he was ready to venture into Boston Wharf to fulfil Pegs' dying wish. This was the least he could do for the man who had protected him many times – sometimes at the risk of his own life – from the fiendish rogues that had blighted the good ship *Endurance*.

At the crack of dawn, Denim began the fifteen mile trek to Boston Wharf. Riding south through miles of rocky hillsides, he eventually came to flatter land and, as the terrain became greener, watered by moist sea breezes, he knew he was nearing the coast. In glorious sunshine, he rode past quaint cottages until he came to the terraced buildings that lined the narrow, cobbled streets of the port town. Boston

Wharf had grown since Pegs' visit, and Denim realized he would have to search for Rosie's Cantina. Even so, he was impelled to go to the harbour first and view the sea.

His approach to the large quayside was greeted by the manic screech of seagulls, the smell of fish as fishermen emptied their nets, and the humdrum clatter of dock workers handling cargoes of imported goods. Schooners, messenger yachts, galleys, and trawlers were all moored, and he glimpsed his first sighting of a steamship. He had heard that these metal vessels were fast becoming the modern way to traverse the oceans, but for him the majestic beauty of the old sailing ships, with their giant canvas sails and towering masts, could never be bettered. And his heart raced when he caught sight of the man o' war anchored out on the brine.

A fleeting thought made him glance up and down the quayside, but there was no sight of the captain's barge or of any redcoats. Perhaps he was worrying unnecessarily. After all these years, surely the British Navy had forgotten him. Dragging himself away from the harbour, he rode up a long, tree lined avenue to a circular road full of shops displaying all manner of goods; clothes, shoes, trinkets, jewellery, weapons, flowers, fruits, and vegetables. On the busy sidewalks, men in bowlers, berets, Stetsons, and sombreros were all going about their daily business, while fashionable dressed ladies, wearing bonnets, hoods, shawls, and scarves, held on to their parasols as they gossiped in small groups.

Fancy two-wheel traps transported sophisticated looking persons to their destinations. Sailors on shore leave searched for the nearest tavern. Dogs barked and chased supply wagons that criss-crossed the rutted road. Noisy children played catch and dared one another to climb the solitary maple tree in a grassy clearing. Beyond a statue of President Lincoln, Denim spotted two red-coated sentinels guarding the doorway of a three storey building. On the eaves, British and American flags stamped their governments' authority. A cavalry sergeant came out of the entrance and, mounting his steed, led a troop of blue coated horse soldiers two by two down the street.

Denim shifted his gaze to the Boston Palace Casino, an impressive white building with wide steps all the way up to its arched doors. This would be a good place to start his search for Katie, he thought. Dismounting, he tethered the horse.

From a dark alleyway on the street, a gaunt, brooding face peered out to watch Denim climb the casino steps. The face growled its displeasure and slunk back into the shadows. On the top floor of the government building, red curtains were snatched aside from the window as two sharp blue eyes focused on Denim entering the Boston Palace. On recognition, two bushy eyebrows lifted in amazement.

Inside the spacious hall, Denim marvelled at the magnificent white staircase spiralling to the first floor. Huge glass chandeliers, hanging from the high ceiling, reflected facets of light in the gilt-edged mirror behind the long mahogany counter. Ladies, dressed in beautiful gowns, held onto the arms of wealthy beaus gambling at crowded blackjack, roulette, and monte tables. Troupes of dancing girls performed on a high stage to the music of the piano and a banjoist.

Leaning against a wooden pillar at the bar, Denim watched the entertainment until the white uniformed waiter served him a drink. When he asked the whereabouts of Rosie's Cantina, the waiter laughed. 'This is Rosie's Cantina, or should I say, it once was. But why do you ask?'

Surprised to have found the cantina so quickly, Denim replied, 'I'm looking for Katie Adams. I believe she used to work here.'

'Wait one moment, sir.' The waiter pulled a velvet curtain to one side, behind the bar, and disappeared through a hidden door. While waiting, Denim examined his image in the bar mirror. His long hair was greying prematurely, he thought, and there were too many lines on his face. They made him look much older than he was. The self-analysis was interrupted when the waiter reappeared. But without speaking to Denim, he went to serve other customers.

Denim was puzzled until an elegant lady, wearing an open-necked white-laced camisa and a sweeping blue dress that reached the parquet flooring, came through the doorway. Silver ringlets of hair fell about her shoulders and the long crystal earrings complemented the stunning gemstone on her cleavage. 'I am Christina Royale and I own the Boston Palace. You have been asking about Katie Adams. Who are you, and what do you want?'

By the authority in her voice, Denim could tell that she was used to being obeyed. Perhaps her wealth had won obedience, but even so, most men would have readily succumbed to her beauty and would have been only too willing to fulfil her wishes. Introducing himself as Mr Armstrong, Denim explained how Pegs had fallen in love with Katie Adams many years ago, and it had been his friend's dying wish for Katie to know why he had never returned to Boston Wharf.

Christina Royale looked sharply at Denim. 'Why has it taken you all these years to come to Boston

Wharf?'

Denim sensed the coldness of her reply, and explained, 'It was impossible for me to honour my friend's dying wish, until now. And only by chance, as I was on my way to do business in a nearby town, did I come across Boston Wharf.'

Christina Royale's emerald-green eyes showed suspicion, so Denim offered the locket from around his neck. Her slender fingers, each adorned with intricate gold rings, opened the locket. As she viewed the portrait, her eyes welled. She dabbed the tears with an embroidered handkerchief, and then she handed the locket back to Denim.

'We were business partners,' said Christina Royale. 'Over the years, Boston Wharf became a very popular port, and flourished into a major trading post. Katie wanted the old cantina gutted and replaced by a modern establishment. I was always worried about taking the risk, but eventually she talked me into it. We arranged a loan from the bank and used all our savings. The result is this beautiful building that you are now standing in. Through Katie's foresight and ambition, the Boston Palace made us both very rich.' Her eyes filled again as she recounted the past. 'Five years ago Katie came down with cholera. She's buried in the cemetery at the east end of town. You can't miss her grave. I paid for the biggest and best headstone available.'

Denim was saddened by the details, but his burning curiosity prompted him to ask, 'Did Katie ever marry?'

Christina Royale smiled as she recalled her friend. 'No, she never did, but Katie had many offers of marriage; she turned them all down. She always told her suitors that a sailor had captured her heart many years ago, and she was waiting for his return. But she never revealed who the love of her life was, not even to me.' Christina Royale wiped away the last tear and returned the handkerchief to her sleeve. 'I trust I have been of some help to you, Mr Armstrong. You did say that was your name?'

'Yes, ma'am. And I must thank you, for confiding in me,' said Denim. Christina gave a courteous nod and disappeared through the curtained door. What to do now, thought Denim – visit the cemetery or ride back to the river? As he lifted his glass to finish his beer, he caught sight of a ghastly face leering at him through the bar mirror. He wheeled around and scanned the crowded room. The evil face was nowhere to be seen. Denim had always thought that his old enemy was dead, but now he was not sure. Perhaps, after discussing the past with Christina Royale, his mind was playing tricks.

A knife whistled through the air. Missing Denim by inches, it embedded into the wooden pillar. He spun around to see the culprit running up the spiral staircase. Grabbing the knife, Denim gave chase. As he pushed through the crowds, ladies screamed and the music stopped. Dancing girls ran off the stage. Bounding up the stairs, he saw the knife thrower disappear through a door. In hot pursuit, Denim crashed into the empty bedroom and, just as the man was climbing out of an open window, he dived at him. Dropping through the air, they hit the ground rolling over. Denim fought his way to the top and sank the blade deep into the man's throat. A fountain of blood shot into the air. Jumping to his feet, Denim stared at the ebony-handled stiletto, and then at the black patch covering the dead man's eye. His revenge list was complete; he had finally killed the fiend who had whipped Jack to death.

The patter of military boots saw Denim surrounded by redcoats. A warrant officer shouted an order and Patch's body was dragged away. Relieved of his firearm, Denim was frogmarched across the grassy clearing and into the government building. Pushed up three flights of steps, by two guards, he was shoved into the judicial courtroom. Rows of chairs half filled the long room as if waiting for a jury. Red curtains draped three tall windows that looked out over the clearing to the Boston Palace Casino. Books and paperwork cluttered a sturdy table.

An oil painting of Queen Victoria decorated the wall above a Georgian mantelpiece. In front of the royal portrait stood a British admiral, dressed in full regalia. His white plumed tricorn hat was pulled well over his forehead, down to the bushy brows and sharp blue eyes. A neatly trimmed black beard covered most of his face. Hanging by his side was the customary brass cutlass.

After all the years of avoiding the sea-ports, Denim was crestfallen to have been captured in one. He knew that if he was to face proceedings for killing Patch, the authorities would soon find out who he was, and he would be deported to England and hanged for treason.

The warrant officer placed Denim's gun belt on the table. After giving his report, he was dismissed along with the two guards and left the room. The Admiral turned his attention to the prisoner. 'Signor, did you know of the man you have just killed?'

'I have never seen the man before today,' replied Denim.

'But signor, if you did not know the man, then why did you kill him?'

'Because he tried to kill me.'

The admiral gave a doubting look. 'If the man did not know you, signor, then why would he try to kill you?'

'I don't know.' Denim knew he did not sound convincing, but that was all he could say.

The admiral stared astutely. 'Then please tell me signor, what is your business in Boston Wharf?'

'I'm just passing through.'

'Umm,' murmured the admiral. 'So, you are just passing through, and someone who doesn't know you tries to kill you?' He raised his bushy eyebrows questioningly. His blue eyes were penetrating. Denim remained silent; he thought it best to say as little as possible. 'Signor, if you are just passing through Boston Wharf, then what is your destination?'

'I'm looking for ranch work, in the next town.'

The admiral stared coldly at Denim. 'Signor, do you know that hanging without a trial is the procedure for the crime you have committed?' There was an uncomfortable silence. The admiral searched Denim's face for some reaction, but there was none. 'Strange as it may be, signor, on this occasion you happen to have done the British realm a favour.' Surprised at the disclosure, Denim wondered what would be said next.

'The man that you have just killed is known as Patch,' said the admiral. 'His proper name is Jim Dulton. He was the leader of the pirates that plundered the merchant ships in the Caribbean, and supplied contraband to the black markets of New Orleans. The British Navy have been trying to capture him for years. And it is for this reason alone, signor, that you are exonerated and free to go.'

Feeling relief, but not showing it, Denim nodded politely and turned to leave. He could not wait to get out of the building. The admiral saw Denim's haste. 'One moment, signor. You have not yet told me your name.'

Denim was caught wrong-footed. His reply was muddled. 'It's Den... er, Danny Colvern.' He tried to sound convincing, but there was a moment's silence as the words hung in the air and both men stared at one another.

The admiral's piercing glare softened, and his black nest of a beard parted to give way to a wry smile. 'Then it is *hasta la vista,* Signor Danny Colvern.'

Denim had just reached the door when the admiral shouted again. This time there was urgency in his voice. 'Signor, your gun.' The admiral pointed to the table where the warrant officer had left the gun belt. Denim could have kicked himself. He had been so anxious to get out of the room that he had forgotten all about the gun.

'Much obliged,' said Denim, as he strapped on the gun belt.

'You must forgive me, Signor Danny Colvern, but you do look familiar to me. Are you sure we have not met before?'

'Positive,' said Denim, a little too curt. This cat-and-mouse game was getting to him.

The admiral came closer. 'But signor, did you not once serve time on the British ship known as the *Endurance*?'

Denim's heart sank. 'I have never been on a ship,' he said as he grabbed the handle of the door. Now that he had the gun, he would take his chances against the guards.

'Ah signor, but I find that you have lied to me. Your name is Denim Armstrong, and I believe that you are wanted by the British Navy for mutiny.'

The words thundered in Denim's head. A sudden blood rush made him pull the gun. He pointed it threateningly at the admiral. But to Denim's astonishment, the officer threw open his arms and came forward in fits of laughter to embrace him. 'My dear Denim, please forgive my silly indulgences, but do you not recognize me under this beard? For it is I, Lieutenant Thorpe.'

Denim was stunned by the revelation, but as the admiral hugged him, he knew it was indeed Lieutenant Thorpe, the officer who had befriended him and Pegs, and who had protected them against Blackie's gang. With tears stinging his eyes, Denim returned the embrace. After all these years, it was wonderful to see the lieutenant again.

When the rejoicing stopped, Denim asked what had happened to the mutineers on that fateful day. 'Men that weren't killed in the harbour,' said the admiral, 'returned to the ship with me. Back in England, the ringleaders were drawn and quartered, and I was made admiral of the fleet.'

'What about Patch?' asked Denim. 'How did he manage to survive on the boat without food and water?'

'Corsairs crossed his path and rescued him. Over the years, news of his whereabouts came from the pirates that we captured. Apparently, Patch killed the captain who had saved his life, and took command of the ship, *The Black Dog*.'

'How did he end up here, in Boston Wharf?' asked Denim.

'Three days ago we came across *The Black Dog*; it had hit a reef and they were bailing out water. Most of the crew were taken prisoner, but Patch and a handful of men escaped in a small boat. We salvaged the contraband on the ship before it sank, and then we came into port. The harbour patrol had shot dead five of the pirates, but Patch escaped into the town. We were unable to find him until he saw you, and came out of hiding. He must have blamed you for his being abandoned on the boat, and wanted revenge.'

'What of Isaac?' asked Denim, 'is he still with you?'

Admiral Thorpe's face tightened. 'Unfortunately, Isaac was the first to board *The Black Dog.* Patch shot him in the face. He died instantly.' Denim was saddened by the news; he had always been fond of the German arm wrestler.

'Now then, Denim, it is your turn. Tell me how you have fared in this vast new country.' Denim told how he had escaped from the harbour, and about the terrible wolf fight. Then he gave a brief history of jobs that he had undertaken, but he left out the robberies, the killings, and the gunfights. Compared to Admiral Thorpe's success, he felt ashamed.

Admiral Thorpe put a friendly hand on Denim's shoulder, 'I have to attend a meeting in this room shortly, with some of the town's elite. Perhaps we could meet again this evening, for a late dinner. I have something very important to tell you.'

'I'm sorry,' said Denim, 'but I have two friends waiting for my return. Perhaps we could rendezvous here, in a week's time.'

'Alas, my dear Denim, that would be impossible, for we set sail in three days. Oh, very well, I must tell you the good news now.' Intrigued, Denim listened carefully. 'Currently, there are uprisings in the four corners of the British Empire; from Maori wars in New Zealand, to South American uprisings in

Venezuela, and now there is unrest in Europe, which may lead to war. The British crown needs to reinforce its armies, and skilled and knowledgeable men like yourself are much needed to lead and train new recruits.'

'But what is the good news?' interrupted Denim.

'Patience, my dear Denim, have patience.' Admiral Thorpe rattled off the information as quickly as possible and then said, 'Because of these pending wars, Her Royal Highness has declared an amnesty to all those in exile. Anyone wishing to return to England may do so, providing they take up a post in the military. This means you can go home, my dear man, and in safety. But it is only by a miracle that we have met now, for the amnesty ends in ten weeks.'

Denim was astonished at the news. 'But how can I get back to England so quickly, and how do I receive the royal pardon?'

'You can sail back to England with me. My ship is anchored just off port. Weather permitting, and with a bit of luck, we should arrive back in England before the deadline.'

The good news was everything that Denim had ever wished for; to go home and see his mother and father, if still alive, and his brothers and sister, who by now must all have families of their own. Admiral Thorpe gave Denim a friendly slap on the back. 'Well, what say you, Denim? This is a chance of a lifetime. To return home and become a free man again.'

Denim was desperate to sail back to England, but after months on the trail with Gus and Kid Rio, he had to consider his loyalty. 'First, I have some urgent business to attend to, but I will be back in time to set sail. What is the name of your ship?'

'*Victorious* – it's the last man o' war in commission. We set sail at nine hundred hours on Wednesday morn. The captain's barge will be moored in the dock.'

'Three days? It's cutting it fine,' said Denim, 'but I will definitely get back in time.' He gave a farewell embrace to his old acquaintance, and ran down the stairs.

Admiral Thorpe signalled the guards to let Denim pass. 'Don't be late Denim, we sail prompt.'

'Wednesday morn,' Denim shouted, as he ran past the two sentinels and across the grassy clearing to Boston Palace Casino. Mounting his horse, he galloped east, towards the cemetery. He had a quest to fulfil.

Finding the largest tombstone in the graveyard, Denim dismounted and read the epitaph.

Katie Adams 1812–1870
God be with you.
Your devoted friend, Christina.

Denim dug a shallow hole by the graveside and buried the gold locket. Looking up to the heavens, he spoke his thoughts aloud. 'Well, old friend, this is the best that I could do for you. I hope now that you are reunited with Katie. The one you loved.' A slight tear blessed Denim's eyes as he remembered Pegs. Then, with thoughts of home and the chance to sail once again on a man o' war, he mounted his horse and rode vigorously back to his two friends, who he hoped were still waiting by the river.

Chapter 23

Hang Tree Falls

It was almost dusk when Denim rode into the camp by the river. Gus and Kid Rio were pleased to see their friend arrive back unscathed and invited him to share the jack rabbit they had caught that morning. Sitting around the small campfire, Denim told his two friends how Katie had died of an illness and then about the fight with Patch, but he said nothing about Admiral Thorpe and the amnesty, or his intentions to sail home to England. He would wait until tomorrow, he thought, after they had settled their business in Hang Tree Falls.

Moving into the shadows, Kid Rio laid on his back and gazed at the stars. He thought about Billy the Kid and wondered how he had earnt the reputation of Fastest Gun Alive. Then he thought about Denim and Gus and how they had saved his life in Kirkdeed Town. Before that, he had never trusted anyone, but Denim had become a father figure to him, and Gus the friend he had never had. They were his family; he must not let them down. Tomorrow, he would kill Billy the Kid. With his hand resting on his gun, he fell asleep.

Gus stretched out beside the fire. After the death of his mother and Old Lon, he had been all alone in the world. When Denim had arrived at the tin mine, he had bonded to him like a sibling would to an older brother. But his thoughts about Kid Rio had changed. The boy killer had turned into a killing machine, with no respect for people whatsoever. Gus hoped that he would be there on the day when someone lowered

Kid Rio's colours, but he knew that tomorrow would be just like all the other gunfights. Billy the Kid would end up in boot hill and Kid Rio's ego would become twice as big. Snuggling under the blanket, Gus was soon snoring.

Resting against a tree, Denim thought about going home, a dream come true; nothing must spoil it. He always worried somewhat before a showdown, and the old-timers' accounts of Billy the Kid came to mind. Some of the stories sounded convincing, but when he remembered how easily Kid Rio had beaten Two-Gun Pete, he knew there was nothing to fear. He glanced at his two sleeping friends. They were a strange pair, he thought. Both had suffered traumatic lives, but instead of showing empathy for one another, they were opposed, and if it had not been for his companionship, he knew that they would have long since parted ways.

In these last few months Kid Rio had become difficult to ride with. The naïve young man that he had once been, was beyond all recognition; Kid Rio was now an evil killer, who always shot to kill and enjoyed doing so. Tomorrow would be a formality, thought Denim; once over, he would ride back to Boston Wharf and sail home to England. As the campfire flickered out, he closed his eyes.

Denim had slept later than he had intended. He could see that Gus and Kid Rio were ready to travel. After refreshing himself in the river, he joined his two friends on the trail. The three men rode in silence. Each had their own thoughts of what might happen in Hang Tree Falls. Ten miles east brought them to a large oak on the outskirts of the town. A muster of carrion crows, disturbed by the riders, became airborne and winged it to the next isolated tree. Startled by the black-winged invasion, a skylark flew vertically into the pale-blue sky and shrieked a warning cry.

Underneath the oak's canopy of leaves, a man dangled from a noose. Face unrecognizable through bird pecking, the cadaver's bare feet were black in death. Around the man's neck hung a message: *Welcome to Hang Tree Falls.* Denim glanced at his two friends. Neither said a word. Kneeing their horses onward, they came to the outbuildings of the town.

A string of mustangs stomped and whinnied inside a corral next to a large barn. Open doors gave view to the blacksmith, bent over the hindquarters of the horse he was re-shoeing. Across the street the Land Survey Office, which doubled as a bank, opened for business as a woman lowered her sunshade and walked in. Adjacent to the bank was the jailhouse. Denim was pleased to see it had been boarded over and was out of use. Riding by shacks, cabins, and lean-tos, the haberdashery and the general food store, they dismounted outside the gunsmith's. Denim slapped his dusty hat against his thighs and took in the surroundings. Only a few people populated the long street, but the tuneful sound of a honky-tonk from the Alamo Saloon, and nine horses at the hitch rail, suggested business as usual.

Denim shifted his gaze to the rhythmic clang of a hammer; an old man was making a coffin from rough-sawn timber. For the poor soul hanging on the tree, thought Denim as he looked beyond the undertaker's. The street tapered into a wagon trail that snaked up a hill, to a small church on the summit. A buckboard was kicking up dust as it rolled down the hillside and into town. With long grey hair streaming behind her, the woman driver cracked the bullwhip over the horse's head and the wagon raced past the trio and down the street. A dog yelped and skittered out of the way as the buckboard skidded to a halt, outside the blacksmith's. Wearing a long trench coat, the woman jumped out of the wagon and dashed inside the barn.

Exchanging glances, the trio crossed the street to the Alamo Saloon and pushed through the bat-wing doors. The music stopped. All heads but one turned to view the newcomers. Eyes quickly adjusting to the shadowy interior, Denim could see his reflection in a sizeable mirror on the wall behind the bar. Bright sunlight streamed through two partially glazed doors at the side of the bar and highlighted the fug of tobacco smoke in the room, as it twirled its way upwards to the nicotine-stained ceiling. A large wagon wheel, with lit candles around its rim, was suspended by ropes tied off at the rafters. The homemade chandelier afforded a brighter ambience to the middle of the room, while oil lamps, fixed intermittently on the timbered walls, created flickering shadows.

Denim ordered drinks from the squat, pug-faced bartender, and the music started again. As three glasses were being filled with the local brew, Denim noticed the bartender was shy of a handgun, but behind him, on a shelf, was a double-barrelled shotgun. Hanging on a hook was the customary wooden mallet, used to part wayward drunks from their money or to discourage rabble-rousers.

A cowpoke standing at the corner of the bar signalled that he was leaving. The bartender, surprised that he was leaving so soon when he normally stayed for a session, called out, 'OK Josh, see you later.' Josh Brown was glad to get out of the saloon. He had recognized the three strangers the moment they had walked in. He remembered the day back in Abilene Town, when a dozen of his friends had been left for dead and, being the only member of the Black Hill Gang to escape that day, he was not going to wait for the trio to recognize him. He pulled his horse from the hitch rail and left town in a hurry.

Denim noticed the young man dressed in black attire standing central to the bar. A black hat rested on his back held by the wind ties around his neck. Strapped low on his thigh, a silver pistol shone out like a jewel. Could he be the Fastest Gun Alive? wondered Denim. He sure looked the part. Two businessmen in pinstriped suits stood at the end of the bar; they weren't packing guns. Deeper in the room, an attractive young woman rattled out tunes on the honky-tonk, while five cowhands played stud poker under the cartwheel of light. In the farthest corner of the room, an old man, hair white as snow, sat with his head on the table, snoring. His dog lay quiet, under the table.

The bartender asked the strangers if they had business in town, or were just passing through, but they picked up their drinks and moved to an empty table. Used to strangers not being talkative, the bartender was not insulted by their silence. Studying the three men, he decided they were not sodbusters, prospectors, wranglers, or even cowpokes; perhaps they were on the run from the law. His thoughts were suddenly interrupted when a rowdy customer came bustling through the doors. 'Huh, the town drunk,' mumbled the bartender.

Frayed suspenders criss-crossed the old man's sweat soaked vest and held up baggy trousers that fell well short of his worn out boots. His gun holster had slid around his waist, and rested on his backside. Staggering up to the bar, his floppy straw hat drooped over his bristled face. 'Service! I want some service!' he hollered.

'All right, Charlie, I've heard you,' shouted the bartender, coming from the other end of the bar. 'Now then, what do you want?'

'Whiskey!' shouted Old Charlie, slavering through the gaps in his teeth.

'Let's see the colour of your money first,' said the bartender.

Old Charlie slapped two coins on the bar. His befuddled gaze fixed on the glass as the bartender poured him whiskey. Amused, Denim watched the old drunk. Then he spotted the gun belts hanging on the adobe wall next to the glazed doors, and the notice board that had a warning:

Firearms not allowed in Molly's kitchen.
Leave your guns on the hooks, or else!
Molly

Denim grinned at the threat and then turned his attention to the card players. Four of the men looked like cowhands. The way they wore their guns suggested that they were used for turning stampedes and killing rattlesnakes out on the trail. But the fifth gambler was different; he was the only man who had not turned around when they had entered the saloon. Wearing a short, open jacket and an expensive Panama hat, he coughed intermittently, drank whiskey, and smoked a cigarillo. A brand new Smith and Wesson was strapped to his right thigh. There was an air of respect from the four cowhands towards this man and, judging by the considerable pile of cash on his side of the table, he was the only one winning.

Old Charlie became noisy again. He had downed the first drink and was demanding more. 'Fill her up,' he spat.

'You've got no money left, Charlie,' shouted the bartender from the other end of the bar, 'It's time to go.' Old Charlie licked the glass dry and then banged it down in anger. Cussing to himself, he stumbled towards the glazed doors.

'Charlie! Hang up your gun belt.' The bartender's shout was wasted. Charlie disappeared into Molly's kitchen.

The bat-wing doors opened and an Indian walked in from the street. Two white-tipped eagle's feathers protruded from the red ribbon around his forehead. Black pigtails of hair hung down each side of his square jaws, while a necklace of wolf's incisors gleamed on his bare red chest. Strapped to his tasselled leggings was a formidable Bowie knife. Deerskin moccasins allowed him to walk quietly to the bar, where a friendly greeting indicated he was a regular visitor.

Anger spiked like molten lava in Gus's chest. Fingers curling around the trigger of his gun, he rose to his feet. 'Hold it,' hissed Denim, as he stayed Gus's hand. 'Don't forget what we're here for.' Gus was burning with anger. He had sworn, many years ago, to kill every Indian he came across; and up till now, he had been true to his word. But to sit only feet away from the object of his hatred it took all of his willpower, and Denim's restraining hand, to stop him from filling the Indian with lead.

'Don't worry, Gus,' chirped Kid Rio, 'I'll help you kill Indians by the wagonload when we're done here.' Gus glowered at his two friends. They did not understand how it was for him. Their lives had not been destroyed by Indians. But he knew Denim was right. Now was not the time. He could wait.

Suddenly, the kitchen doors banged wide open. The music stopped and everyone turned to see Old Charlie, arms flailing, crash in a heap in the middle of the saloon floor. In the kitchen doorway stood a goliath of a man. A large black chain hung around his bull neck and disappeared under a loose poncho that stretched down to his knees. Through overgrown locks of black hair, he glared menacingly. Then lowering his head under the frame of the door, he entered the room. Behind him tiptoed a skinny, Chinese manservant dressed in a baggy white top and trousers.

Bleary eyed, Old Charlie recovered to a sitting position. Knowing the violent reputation of his attacker, he was unsure whether to get up and run; instead he sat there like a meek animal caught in the path of a deadly predator. The giant thrust one hand high above his head. The bartender knew the signal well. He unhooked the mallet from behind the bar and threw it precisely towards the outstretched hand. Snatching the hammer out of the air, the giant moved towards his victim.

Fear of death sobered Old Charlie. Too late, he scrambled to his feet. With devastating force, the mallet crashed down on his skull. In a pool of blood, Old Charlie sagged to the floor. As the body twitched in spasms of death, the giant stared indifferently at his kill, then he slung the blunt weapon back to the bartender. 'Get rid of the body,' he growled.

'OK Molly,' said the bartender as he wiped the mallet clean and placed it back on the hook. Molly lowered his head to go through the glazed doors and, like a giant grizzly returning to its cave after destroying an intruder, he disappeared into the kitchen. Shuffling behind, the Chinese servant followed his master. Seconds later, the straw hat came skimming through the air and landed on top of Old Charlie's lifeless body. The kitchen doors slammed shut.

Denim looked at his two friends. 'So, that's Molly.' Gus and Kid Rio nodded their surprise. They too had expected Molly to be a woman.

'Hey, Doc,' shouted the bartender to the gambler wearing the Panama hat. 'Do you want to take a look at the body before we move it outside?'

With a wave of his hand, the fancily dressed gambler declined, then he pulled a neckerchief from his pocket to stifle a coughing bout. When the affliction subsided, he signalled the cowhand to resume dealing. Seeing the gambler respond to the name of Doc, Denim wondered if the man was the notorious Doc Holliday, the rogue dentist who had turned killer at the gambling tables, and who had reputedly shot many a man for cheating. Rumour had it that he was slowly dying from a lung infection.

After carrying Old Charlie outside, the bartender and the Indian lifted the body onto horseback ready to be taken to the undertakers. From a second horse, the Indian removed a dead pronghorn, and chucking the wild animal across his shoulders, he carried it into Molly's kitchen. Returning to the bar room, the bartender sprinkled sawdust on the blood slick and then carried on working behind the counter as if nothing had happened.

Stunned by witnessing a brutal murder, the saloon girl was ready to walk out of her job. She remembered how destitute she had been when she had

185

arrived by stagecoach, a week ago, and how finding work in the saloon had been her saviour, but now she was ready to quit. She approached the bar.

Guessing the saloon girl's problem, the bartender growled, 'Go play the honky. That's what you're getting paid for.'

'After what I've just seen, I don't know why I'm still here.' Her face became ashen. She held onto the bar.

Thinking the girl was going to faint, the bartender opened a bottle of whiskey and poured a generous portion into a glass. 'This will help.' His voice mellowed. 'But you'd better go and make some music. If Molly doesn't hear the honky-tonk, he's likely to come out here again and there's no telling what he might do.'

She choked a little on the drink as she tried to make her mind up, but the only other work in town was the whorehouse and she could never resort to that seedy way of life. The two businessmen felt sorry for the saloon girl. They had arrived in town only that morning to register a land purchase at the surveyor's office and, after signing a contract, they had decided to celebrate in the Alamo. Having no knowledge of the saloon's pugnacious reputation, the last thing they expected was to witness a violent killing. One of them beckoned the bartender over. 'Listen here my friend, shouldn't someone go and fetch the sheriff?'

'There's no sheriff in this town,' said the bartender bluntly, 'and if I were you, I'd keep my mouth shut and mind my own business.'

'But that poor old man, he didn't stand a chance, and...' His words tailed off as the bartender arrogantly moved away to serve one of the cowhands who had come to the bar. At that moment, the Indian came out of the kitchen and left the saloon. Denim was pleased to see him go. He did not know how much longer he could contain Gus.

The bat-wing doors opened again, and a tall, robust man entered the saloon. 'That's all we need,' grumbled the bartender to himself, 'Jake McCarty, the town bully.' Denim noted the yellow stripes down dark blue pants and the Colt .44 strapped to the man's waist. They suggested ex-military. His green shirt unbuttoned to the waist displayed an admirable physique that was marred only by the white, jagged scar across his chest. Three claw marks, still blood-red on his cheek, and a bulbous nose which had been broken more than once, denoted a troublemaker. The tall man gave a wide berth to the man in black, and moved farther along the bar.

Instinct told the saloon girl that the big man was headed in her direction. She picked up her drink and moved back towards the honky-tonk. As Jake grabbed her by the arm, she tossed the whiskey into his face. Jake howled with laughter and pulled the saloon girl closer. 'Hey, Jake!' protested the cowhand at the bar. 'She's done nothing wrong.'

'Is that so?' Jake scoffed. 'Well, all I want to do is give this little missy a good time.' His strong arms circled her waist. Reeling her in, he tried to kiss her.

A stern voice thundered from the bar. 'Let her go, Jake!'

Jake stared at the double-barrelled shotgun pointing in his direction. Then he threw his head back and guffawed as loud as a jackal. But when he heard the firing pins click into place, he knew the bartender was not bluffing. He hurled the saloon girl to the floor. Then, in a show of defiance, he slammed both hands on the bar and demanded a beer. The bartender released the firing pins and placed the shotgun on the shelf, but within easy reach. Then he poured two beers, one for Jake and one for the cowhand. 'On the house,' declared the bartender, trying to calm the incident.

The cowhand helped the saloon girl to her feet and back to the honky-tonk. When he came to the bar Jake had drunk both beers. 'Hey! What the hell!' snapped the cowhand. But he knew he would come off second best against an ex-army champion boxer.

Another beer was poured for the cowhand, but Jake grabbed that one too. The humiliation proved too much. With both fists flying, the cowhand knocked the pot out of Jake's hand and attacked him. Sidestepping the blows, Jake delivered a right cross that sent the cowhand crashing to the floor and spitting teeth. Before Jake could follow up, the cowhands at the table jumped to their feet and drew their guns.

'That's enough for one day, Jake,' said the bartender. 'Let's have you gone,'

Jake stared at the guns pointing at him. 'All right, I'm leaving,' he growled. 'But I'll get even. I'll get even with you all.' Grabbing the opened bottle of whiskey off the bar, he swigged the contents and moved towards the exit.

Suddenly, the card table overturned. The Panama hat fell to the floor. A shot from the Smith and Wesson shattered the bottle. Jake froze as the whiskey drenched his chest. Denim looked around to see who was so handy with a gun, and was amazed. The gambler named Doc was in fact a beautiful woman. Long auburn hair, which had been contained under the Panama hat, in a bun, now fell loosely over her shapely bosom. She stood in all her glory, blood-red lips and high cheekbones, aiming the gun at Jake.

When Jake saw Belle Starr holding the gun, he could have guessed, she was the only one with the nerve. He touched the deep scratches on his face. Only days ago, she had attacked him for beating up two hired hands on her parents' ranch and, after being forced off the land at gunpoint by Belle Starr's father, Jake had sworn revenge. Seeing the Treble-T ranch horses tethered outside the Alamo, Jake had thought that now was a good time to settle an old score. He had entered the saloon hoping to find Belle Starr's father inside, but instead, it was Belle Starr who was now pointing a gun at him.

'Your father owes me money,' growled Jake.

'The next time you touch one of my men,' spat Belle Starr, 'I will kill you!'

'Your father forced me off the ranch without any pay. He owes me. And if I don't get paid, he'll be dead and you along with him.'

'When my father hears about this, you'll be run out of town for good. Now get the hell out of here before I let loose another round of bullets!' Jake knew if he riled her any further, she would use the gun. He moved towards the exit. While the cowhands righted the table and picked up the cards and money, Belle Starr holstered the Smith and Wesson and recovered her hat.

One of the businessmen whispered nervously, to his colleague, 'I'm getting out of here, while the going's good.'

'And I'm coming with you,' was the reply. Both men drank up and followed in Jake's footsteps, towards the exit.

The fun was over, thought Kid Rio, and decided to have another beer. Crossing the room to the bar he slipped on the blood slick and stumbled into Jake McCarty. Pushed violently backwards, Kid Rio was sent rolling head over heels. Like a wildcat, he sprang to his feet; gun in hand. Teeth gritted in fury, he ran forward and rammed the barrel of the gun into Jake's belly. 'Now then, big man,' he screamed, 'on your knees!' Jake was speechless. Who was this man? One minute he was rolling on the floor and the next, he was pointing a gun. Who was he? Jake knew the only chance of staying alive was to obey the stranger's command. He knelt down.

The bartender had noted the cavalry-twist draw, and the speed of its execution. There was only one man renowned for this unusual method of quick draw and he knew, now, that he was in the presence of the legendary gunslinger Kid Rio.

Chapter 24

Grand Finale

Stuck in the middle of the room, just a few steps behind Jake McCarty, the two businessmen feared to go one way or the other. The saloon girl was pleased to see Jake McCarty being put in his place, but she did not want to witness another killing. She looked over to the bar for some instruction as to what to do, but the bartender was immersed in his own thoughts. He had thought about reaching for the shotgun, but after deciding that the stranger was the infamous Kid Rio, he excused himself from any action at all.

In the silence of the room, the glazed doors creaked open and a blond haired boy came out of the kitchen. Wearing a long grey vest and ripped jeans, he looked fourteen, perhaps fifteen years of age. He recognised the man kneeling on the floor and made a sudden grab for the gun belts hanging on the wall. A bullet exploded near his fingers. 'Don't do it, boy,' said Gus, pointing his gun.

Knelt on the floor, Jake McCarty shouted, 'Do what he tells you, William. Just do what he tells you.'

'OK Pa,' said the boy quietly.

Kid Rio perked up. 'So this is your Pa. Well, you're just in time to say goodbye.' He aimed the shiny black gun at Jake's face.

'No! No!' yelled the boy, tears streaming down his pasty face. Kid Rio lowered the gun. He was enjoying the moment. Jake McCarty knew that the reprieve would be short. While serving time as a sergeant in the U.S. Cavalry, his regiment had often been deployed to rid towns of vigilantes, and he could tell that the killer before him was one of the worst kinds. Except for a miracle, Jake knew his days were numbered; his only wish was that his son would be spared. Tingling sensations prompted Kid Rio to pull the trigger. Again, he levelled the gun at Jake's head.

'Drop it!' came a loud voice from the bar. The man in black was aiming the silver pistol at Kid Rio. Kid Rio cursed himself for not being more vigilant. If this was the Fastest Gun Alive, then there was not much chance of outshooting him, not while he held the advantage. He let the shiny black gun drop back inside its holster. And then he waited for the man holding the silver pistol to make a mistake; just one little mistake.

'Tell your friend to drop his gun too,' said the man in black, 'or you're a dead man.' Kid Rio remained silent, and Gus kept hold of the gun. Stalemate, thought Denim, if the man in black shoots Kid Rio, then Gus would shoot the man in black. Unexpectedly, the kitchen doors kicked wide open. Molly entered the room. He could see the local fast gun, who he had hired only that morning, was pointing a silver pistol at the stranger. Since gold had been found in the canyon, Molly's workload in the kitchen had more than doubled, so he had employed the gunslinger to sort out the drunken fights of the miners in the saloon.

Molly thrust one hand high. The mallet came flying through the air. Snatching hold of the weapon Molly moved threateningly towards Kid Rio. Unexpectedly, the bat-wing doors flew open with a loud clatter. All heads turned to see the return of the Indian. The diversion was all that Kid Rio needed. The gun flew into his hand. Successive shots sent the man in black reeling against the bar, and Jake

McCarty flat-out onto his back. Two more shots hammered into Molly's gut. The Indian's Bowie knife came flying across the room; missing Kid Rio by inches it buried deep into the businessman's throat. A blaze of gunfire from Gus slammed the Indian through the bat-wing doors and onto the street. Quick fire from Denim, exploded the oil lamp above the bartender's head as he made a grab for the shotgun. In a shower of flames the bartender tossed the shotgun onto the bar. Pieces of adobe exploded out of the wall as a shot from Gus stopped the boy from getting a gun. Molly was still advancing. Hammer held high, he was ready to strike. Kid Rio fired the last two bullets. Molly's arm lowered to his side. The mallet dropped to the floor. Then like a giant redwood being felled, he toppled full length. Motes of dust rained from the rafters, as the room shook from the impact.

Quickly, Kid Rio reloaded the gun. Now, he would show them all who they were dealing with. He twirled the shiny black gun on his finger and flipped it back into its holster. Then with the speed and accuracy that he had always known, he drew the gun and triggered two shots. In a spectacular display of sparks the shotgun flew off the bar. Brimming with confidence, he looked at the carnage. Molly was face down among overturned furniture. Jake McCarty was spread-eagled on the floor. Against the bar, the man in black had died in a sitting position. Underneath the bat-wing doors, the dead Indian could be seen on the street. The businessman was kneeling beside his dead partner. In the corner of the room, the white-haired old man was still sleeping, the dog lying quietly by his feet. Belle Starr and the cowhands had not moved from the table. Sat by the honky-tonk, the saloon girl was looking at the Chinese servant cowering near the kitchen door.

Kid Rio was back in control, thought Denim; there would be no more surprises. He holstered his gun and looked across at the man dressed in black slumped against the bar. So that was Billy the Kid, the so-called Fastest Gun Alive. Now Kid Rio had proven himself once again, they could leave. When they reached the huge granite boulder that divides the trail, Denim would tell his two friends that he was sailing back to England. His thoughts of home were interrupted when he heard Kid Rio shouting at the boy.

'So you tried to get a gun, did you, sonny?' Kid Rio's lips curled with hate as he levelled the shiny black gun at the boy.

'Aw, let the boy alone,' said Gus, 'there's no need.' Killing young boys wasn't Gus's way. Killing damn Indians yes, but not young boys.

'He's been asking for it,' snapped Kid Rio. Gus felt strongly about saving the boy's life, but he knew that Kid Rio had no qualms about killing, be it man, woman, or child. Gus thought about challenging him, but he knew he would lose. He glanced at Denim for support.

Not wanting anything to spoil the chance of sailing back to England, Denim was reluctant to interfere. And he hoped Gus had the same sense, for whenever Kid Rio held that gun in his hand he was like a man possessed. They had both witnessed Kid Rio's hard-hearted cruelty latterly; when enraged, he was a killer without a conscience.

With no back-up from Denim, Gus pleaded with Kid Rio one more time. 'At least, let the boy get a gun.' Gus knew the boy had no chance, but that was all he could do for him.

Kid Rio's cruel lips parted in a mischievous grin; he liked the idea. 'OK sonny, you wanted to get a gun. Take your pick.' He waved his firearm in the direction of the gun belts on the wall. Cautiously, the boy reached out with his left hand and took a gun belt from the rack. Kid Rio's voice deepened, 'Now strap it on, and let's see if you can do better than your old man did.'

The young boy slung the belt smoothly around his waist. The buckle snapped crisply into place as the gun came to rest upon his left thigh. Immediately, the dog was up on all fours barking wildly at the boy. Awakened by the dog, the white-haired old man gave a sharp tug on the rope and the barks were stifled into menacing growls. Hair bristled on its neck; its head lowered and ears flattened; its hind legs stiffened, ready to attack. The old man yanked the rope tighter and the animal was choked into silence.

How strange, thought Denim; the dog had lazed quietly during the shootout, but now that the boy had strapped the gun on, it was going wild. Aware that some animals, especially dogs, have a sixth sense, he wondered what had spooked it. Denim also noticed that the boy had not taken the nearest gun, but had chosen one from the far end of the rack. This must be the boy's very own, he thought, which again was most unusual. Although boys out west were taught how to use a gun from an early age, their parents did not usually allow them to wear a six-shooter until they were much older. But most surprising of all to Denim was how easily the boy had strapped on the heavy gun belt. And now he was wearing it, he no longer looked afraid. And yet here he was, facing the deadliest gunfighter the west had ever known.

Scanning the room, Denim searched for answers.

Belle Starr and the four cowhands had all put their hands flat out on the card table. The bartender too had put his hands flat on top of the bar. Even the old man, who had slept throughout the gunplay, was now sat bolt upright with both hands on the table. What was going on? Denim could not fathom it. And why was no one coming to the boy's rescue, when earlier they had all supported the saloon girl against Jake McCarty?

Oblivious to Denim's worries, Kid Rio carried on teasing the boy. 'I'm going to give you a chance, sonny. I am going to let you draw first.' Kid Rio holstered the shiny black gun and folded his arms. He waited for the boy's reaction, but all he received was a blistering stare. It brought back bad memories of Scrapper, the school bully; he used to stare like that just before attacking. All the hatred that had ever been instilled in Kid Rio as a child resurfaced. He decided to kill everyone in the saloon, except his two friends.

Slowly, he became aware of an icy cold stillness in the room. Something was wrong. He knew that silence always preceded a gun duel, but somehow this silence was different. And there was an air of expectation on the onlookers' faces, as if they were waiting for some miracle to happen. He glanced across the room at the boy. Strong sunlight through the glazed doors had created a golden aura around the boy's profile, and in the dimly lit room he looked almost god-like. Tears that had stained his pasty face had been wiped and a grim smile now played around his lips.

The oddness of the moment made Kid Rio doubtful. What was happening? He touched the gun for reassurance. Panic surged through his body. There was no tingling sensation and no warm glow. He gripped the handle tighter; the cold steel made him tremble. Was this the moment he had always feared, when the gun would lose its strange power? For the first time since taking ownership, he felt vulnerable. He tried to boost his self-esteem. Had not everyone been amazed at his speed and accuracy with the gun? Only moments ago, he had shot dead the giant Molly and the town bully Jake McCarty, and the renowned Fastest Gun Alive, Billy the Kid. The boy should be terrified; he was about to die.

A prominent vein on Kid Rio's temple began to throb. Sweat beaded on his forehead. His hands became clammy. His heart pounded against his ribs. He thought of all the men that he had matched in gunfights and wondered if they had experienced these very same feelings just before he had killed them. He shuddered at the thought. But as the boy's cold blue eyes speared right through him, he knew it was the look of death.

Unknown fear made Kid Rio draw. A blaze of gunfire from across the room lifted Kid Rio off his feet and crashing to the floor. Gus was catapulted out of his chair. Blood oozed through the mustard-coloured waistcoat. In that fraction of time the boy had drawn, fired, and holstered. Denim had only managed to grab the handle of his own gun and his two friends were dead. It went against all his powers of reasoning – a boy had beaten Kid Rio. Then a sudden rush of logic hit him; they had all put their hands in view because they knew that the boy was a wizard with the gun. It was their way of saying, 'We're taking no part.' But why had the boy not killed him? Then Denim realized he was next, and everyone was waiting for the grand finale. Denim weighed up his chances: although he was slower than

Kid Rio, he was much faster than Gus and, with his hand already on the butt of the gun, he had an advantage. In reality, he knew that unless Lady Luck dealt some miraculous cards of fate, he too was facing certain death, but there were no options. He would have to take a chance. His grip tightened on the gun.

'William!' A woman's voice screeched over the bat-wing doors.

The distraction was all the luck Denim had hoped for. He pulled the gun. Two shots boomed from across the room. Blood spurted from Denim's shoulder. His gun fell to the floor. He sagged back into the chair. The boy had beaten him.

Chapter 25

The Last Man Standing

Martha barged through the bat-wing doors. Brushing the long grey hair away from her haggard face, she stepped inside the saloon. Her son had left home that morning without her permission. She knew he did odd jobs for the surveyor and the blacksmith, but when she heard gunfire, she jumped into the buckboard and rode fast to the Alamo Saloon. She poked Jake McCarty's dead body with the tip of her bootee. 'Scum!' she scowled, remembering the night fifteen years ago when he had crept through the bedroom window at the smallholding, two miles out of town, and raped her at knifepoint. She recalled his screams of terror when she had ripped the knife across his bare chest while he was in a drunken stupor. And how she had lashed him with the bullwhip as he escaped on horseback.

Nine months later, Belle Starr had helped her with the birth of her only child. Martha knew the trauma had scarred her mentally, for whenever she looked at her son she despised him because he reminded her of Jake McCarty. In the early years she had prevented William from seeing his father, but as the boy grew older, he began to idolize him.

Martha spat on Jake's body, then turning to her son she pointed to the bat-wing doors. 'Get out!' William stood defiant. After seeing his mother defile his father's body, he wanted to kill her. Martha pushed her long trench coat to one side and released the coiled bullwhip hanging on her belt. 'Get out now, or else!'

William knew only too well what would happen if he disobeyed. The tell-tale scars on his legs and back could testify to her cruelty. Governed by years of brutal authority, he let the gun slide back into its holster. Evil thoughts played out in his mind as he moved towards the exit. He knew that one day he would exact revenge on his mother, and that day was getting closer.

With the leather handle of the bullwhip, Martha struck William hard across the face. Blood gushed from his cheekbone. She grabbed hold of his vest and pulled him through the bat-wing doors. A loud 'Heehaw' and a sharp crack of the whip sent the buckboard speeding out of town; up the hillside, by the church, towards home.

Denim was weak from loss of blood. Slumped in the chair, the last few moments had seemed like a nightmare to him. Who could have believed that Kid Rio would meet his match here, in this insignificant little town? Yes, the boy was fast, all right. A born natural. You could practise forever with a gun and never achieve that kind of speed. He looked at Gus sprawled on the floor. If only they had bypassed Kirkdeed Town and carried on up north to the gold rush. They would have had different lives. They might even have struck gold. A searing pain roused him; the bullet in his shoulder had gone deep. He stemmed the flow of blood with his hand, and then he remembered the boy had fired twice. Had the second shot missed? He forced a glance around the room; everyone was staring at him.

In a feeble voice, Denim asked, 'Who was that boy?'

The bartender took it on himself to answer and came closer. 'That boy was William H. Bonney. The townsfolk know him as William H. McCarty, but the boy is better known as Billy the Kid. Surely you've heard of him?' he gloated.

Denim's breathing started to labour. His thoughts became cloudy. His eyes closed, and his head drooped. Wanting Denim to know who had shot him, the bartender repeated the message a little louder. 'Billy the Kid shot you. Can you hear me? Billy the Kid!'

The name pierced Denim's brain like sharp needles. His eyes fluttered open. So it was the boy. The boy was Billy the Kid. Fresh hot blood trickled down Denim's neck. The boy's second shot had not missed; with pinpoint accuracy it had nicked the jugular vein. Denim forced himself out of the chair. The exertion caused the vein to open and, like a breach in a dam wall, the blood poured out. Uncontrollable fear took hold of Denim as he tried to stop the flow. He held out his hand and begged for help. No one responded. His words became incoherent as gurgles of blood spilled from his mouth. Images began to blur. Sounds became muffled. The room started to spin. His legs buckled and he collapsed to the floor. In the last flickers of consciousness, the name Billy the Kid reverberated over and over in his mind. And as the warm, red liquid of life escaped his body, his breathing stopped. Denim was dead.

Chapter 26

The Pinkertons

Sat in the far corner of the room, the white-haired old man rubbed the half-moon scar on his cheek and mumbled how foolish they had all been. He was not sure how many were dead, for in these later years his eyesight was failing. Although he was pleased he had given up that way of life years ago, he had now become a vagrant, roaming aimlessly about the country begging for food and sleeping anywhere.

He picked up the old Spanish black hat which had rested out of sight on the chair next to him and placed it on his head. Although the silver coins on the hatband were tainted and pitted, they still sparkled whenever a ray of light played upon them. He gave a deep sigh for the memories of his misspent youth. Then, pulling the dog by its leash, he weaved his way through the upturned furniture towards the exit.

Being superstitious, he kissed the small rabbit's foot dangling on the silver chain fastened to his shirt before stepping over the dead bodies. He failed to see the shiny black gun on the floor. And he would never have guessed that the body he had just stepped over was the very same tousled-haired youngster that he had given the Devil Gun to, all those years ago back in Rialto Town. Pleased to get outside, away from the chaos, he wandered off with the only friend he had left in the world and the only thing that mattered to him: his faithful dog.

Although the saloon girl was relieved that the fighting was over, she decided to give the job up. She approached the bar for her wages. 'I'm quitting,' she said to the bartender. 'It's the most grisly hour of saloon life I've ever encountered. I've never seen so many killings. I'm getting out now, while *I'm* still alive.'

Ignoring her rant, the bartender grabbed another bottle of whiskey and, as if drink was the answer to everything, he shoved it into her hands. He retrieved the shotgun and placed it on the shelf, then he went to tend to Molly. As he knelt to the floor, Molly gave out a loud groan. 'Hey,' shrieked the bartender, 'Molly's still alive!'

The cowhands helped to roll Molly over onto his back, while Belle Starr pushed the poncho up to inspect the bullet wounds. 'What the hell is this?' she cried. Underneath the poncho was a blue satin vest, made up of small, steel, oblong plates overlapping one another, and riveted to a leather lining. A three-clawed lion had been embossed in gold on the front of the armour. The Chinese servant had given the brigandine vest to Molly, in gratitude for his employment, and he had always insisted that it would bring good fortune. Molly believed the ancient artefact was valuable, and had worn it at all times underneath the poncho.

Removing the heavy chain from around Molly's neck, two cowhands carried the armoured vest to the nearest table. Belle Starr poured whiskey over the belly wounds and, while the cowhands restrained Molly, she probed his bloody flesh with her fingers. Each time a bullet was pulled out, Molly howled with pain and threatened to kill everybody. The last piece of lead was lodged well inside the fat, and Belle Starr had to dig deep. As the bullet was extracted, Molly gave a horrendous cry and threw the cowhands off. Belle Starr jumped out of reach. Grabbing the bottle of whiskey she took a large gulp. 'The ungrateful pig,' she yelled. 'He'll be OK though. I guess the armoured vest saved his life.'

Molly struggled to his feet. He threw the mallet back to the bartender and told him to get rid of the bodies. Then, with one hand, he scooped the heavy armoured vest off the table and strode ponderously back to the kitchen. Like a faithful poodle, the Chinese servant trailed behind.

The bartender and the cowhands were about to move the dead bodies outside when they heard the thunder of galloping hooves and snorting horses. Twelve men dressed in white duster coats and holding Winchester rifles burst through the bat-wing doors. A young chisel-faced man, sporting a handlebar moustache and wearing a Pinkerton badge, strode to the front. 'What the hell's happened here?' He had seen the dead Indian on the street, but he had not expected the death toll inside. 'Pancho, give me the wanted posters.'

'OK Pat,' said the tall Mexican man wearing a large sombrero. He pulled a bundle of papers out of his charro jacket and handed them over.

Pat examined the first cadaver propped against the bar. The man had died in a sitting position, and looked as if he was just waiting to be pulled to his feet. A single shot to the heart had killed him instantly. Pat checked the firing chamber on the silver pistol; it had not been fired. He dropped the firearm onto the dead man's legs, and thumbed through the posters. 'Yep, we've got a match here. Sam Keeler's the name. There's no bounty money though. He's just a two-bit hired gun. Leave him here.'

The next body had been shot in the head. Pat noticed the three scratches on the man's face, and the knife scar across his chest. The army Colt was still holstered. 'No show on the posters,' said Pat, 'leave him here.' Squatting down on the heels of his boots, he looked at three bodies lying close together. 'This one's Gus Stone, the Indian killer. There's seven thousand dollars on his head. Pat read aloud from the next poster. 'And this one here is the Mormon boy. Davy Mathew Joshua Morton, alias Kid Rio. He's worth fifteen thousand. At the last count, twenty-seven deaths were attributed to him. Uh... a religious kid at that. What makes them turn, eh?'

'Is it true he killed his mother and father, and half the school kids in town?' Pancho asked.

'They reckon so,' said Pat. But he knew that most stories were exaggerated, and by the time an outlaw was ever caught, he would be blamed for everything, from killing a cat, to dynamiting a whole town.

The next body had a shoulder wound, but Pat could see that it was the bullet to the neck that had been fatal. 'There's no mistaking Denim Armstrong, men. The picture on the poster is good. He's the leader of the Kirkdeed Trio and there's twenty thousand dollars on his head. Pat read out the long history of crimes. 'Horse thief, cattle rustling, bank robbery, killings; he's wanted in most states, and he's even wanted by the British Navy for mutiny.

Pat gazed at the three dead men. 'Looks like someone's done our job for us,' he said. He felt a certain sadness as he wondered what kind of lives these men had endured, to turn them into wanton outlaws. Then, returning to the sharpness of the lawman that he was, he yelled, 'Get these three bodies strapped on horses, pronto! They're the ones we've been chasing for the last seven months.'

Belle Starr and the saloon girl helped the businessman, who was still in a state of shock, to a chair, while Pancho pulled the Bowie knife out of the dead businessman's throat. 'I guess the Bowie knife belonged to the Indian,' said Pancho as he handed it over to Pat.

Pat questioned everyone about what had happened, but only the saloon girl was willing to talk. She blamed the killings on a young boy who lived with his mother on a smallholding two miles out of town. Pat found the account hard to believe. The Kirkdeed Trio were hardened outlaws, and most men would have failed against any one of them, let alone a young boy. Even so, Pat intended to visit Martha's ranch on the way out. He was curious to see the boy.

A huge shadow blocked the sunlight through the glazed doors as Molly entered the room. Taken aback by the size of the giant man, the posse lifted their rifles in defence. Molly was no help to Pat's enquiries; all he would say was that he was the owner of the saloon, and the Chinese servant could not speak English. Pat turned to the bartender. 'We're leaving four bodies here. If there's no kin, the state will pay for the burials, but there's no funds for the Indian. I'll wire you the money from my office in Kentucky.' The bartender nodded agreement.

Pat shouted to Pancho, 'Are we ready to go?'

'Yo!' replied the Mexican.

As the posse filed out of the saloon, one of the men lagged behind. He picked up the shiny black gun, which he had covertly kicked out of sight, and hid it inside his shirt. Then he joined the troop outside. Pat dropped the Bowie knife on top of the dead Indian and, after checking that the three dead bodies were securely tied to the horses, he mounted his steed and led the entourage out of town. As they rode up the hillside and by the church, Pat thought of how he had nearly given up the search for the outlaws, until they had come across Josh Brown out on the trail. Josh Brown had told them that the Kirkdeed Trio were in the saloon at Hang Tree Falls. He had recognized them from Abilene Town, where they had left more than a dozen people dead. He said he had no intention of being in the Alamo Saloon when the trouble started, and he had got out as fast as he could. With that information, Pat and the posse had ridden hard to Hang Tree Falls.

While the cowhands helped the bartender to drag the three dead bodies out of the saloon and into the street next to the Indian, one of the men went to fetch the undertaker's wagon.

'Who's going to pay for the Indian's burial?' queried one of the cowhands. 'He's got no kin, he lived alone in the wilds.'

'The Indian's horses will fetch a price,' said the bartender, 'and that'll be more than enough for a box and the gravedigger.'

Leaving the cowhands to load the undertaker's wagon, the bartender retreated to the saloon. He sat down and poured himself a glass of whiskey. 'What a day,' he sighed. 'We can do without any more days like this one.' Glad that it was all over, he took a large gulp of whiskey and settled back in the chair and enjoyed the quiet. Little could he have known then that an even bigger bloodbath was on its way to Hang Tree Falls – and that nothing could be done to stop it.

Chapter 27

New Owner for the Devil Gun

As the golden sky morphed into a red sunset, the posse trooped in single file across the high plains. The man who had stolen the shiny black gun was anxious to examine it, but he was fearful of Pat, who did not allow any of his deputized men to pilfer from dead bodies. Without anyone noticing, he manoeuvred his horse to the back of the line and, when the gap had widened between him and the last rider of the posse, he pulled the gun out of his shirt. As he examined it, a slight tingling sensation moved up his arm and a warm sense of well-being coursed through his body. He felt good.

Pat stopped the entourage at a fork in the trail. Which way to go; Martha's ranch or straight back to Pinkerton base? As he pondered, he saw that one of the men had lagged far behind. 'Pancho! Who's that, way back yonder?'

'It's Jesse,' said Pancho.

'Him again,' said Pat. 'What's he up to this time? Send somebody back for him. If he can't keep up with us, we're leaving him behind, and he'll lose his share of the bounty.'

Pancho turned in the saddle and yelled to the rear of the troop, 'Cole! Cole Younger!'

'Here!' shouted Cole.

'Go fetch your friend,' ordered Pancho. 'If he doesn't get back here pronto, he loses his share of the reward money, savvy?'

'Yo!' Cole rode at a pace. As he closed in on his friend, he shouted to him. Not knowing who the rider was, Jesse hid the gun inside his shirt.

Cole's horse stomped to a halt. 'Jesse, if you don't come quick, Pat's going to split your share of the bounty with the rest of the men.'

'Look at this, Cole,' said Jesse as he pulled the gun out of his shirt. 'Have you ever seen such a gun? Look how it glistens.'

'Where'd you get it?'

'Back there, in the saloon.'

'If Pat sees it, he'll kick you out of the posse for sure. He doesn't like anybody stealing things. And if we don't get back to the posse right now, we will both lose our share of the reward money.'

The crimson sunset lit up Jesse's face. His eyes glowed like burning coals of fire. As if in a trance, he slowly raised the gun and pointed it at Cole. His hand began to shake as if he was trying to resist pulling the trigger. 'Jesse! Jesse! What are you doing?' screamed Cole. He knew his friend liked to play pranks, but this was going too far. Spooked by the antic, Cole raced back to the posse. Then, as if a spell had been broken, Jesse lowered the shiny black gun. Bewildered by the strange tingling sensations, and the compulsion to shoot his friend, he stuffed the gun inside his shirt and joined the rest of the men.

'Are you with us, then?' Pat shouted from the head of the troop.

'Aye!' shouted Cole Younger.

'Yo!' yelled Jesse James.

Chapter 28

Death Rides to Hang Tree Falls

Pat was about to lead the troop down the trail to Martha's ranch, when a rider from that direction came trotting towards them. A young boy astride a bay mare slowed to walking pace and greeted them with a big beaming smile. 'Howdy, misters,' he said chirpily.

'Howdy yourself,' said Pat. He noticed the boy was not wearing a gun, and he had a nasty cut across his cheek. 'Where are you off to, boy?'

'I'm going into town to pick up a parcel for my Ma.'

'How did you cut your face?'

'Oh, it's nothing,' said the boy laughing. 'Climbing trees I guess.'

Pat scrutinized the baby face. Not much more than fourteen years of age, he guessed. The boy's striking blue eyes were hypnotic, his smile infectious. 'I take it your name is William?'

'Sure is mister, but how'd you know that?' His broad grin showed off his milky white teeth. Not waiting for an answer, he carried on talking. 'I live at the ranch up yonder, just Ma and me. Call in and see Ma if you like, I'm sure she would make you all welcome. Probably give you a bite to eat, if I know her.' He giggled. Pat could not help thinking how pleasant the boy was.

'Right now, I've got to pick up a parcel,' said the boy, 'and if I don't get back in time for supper, I'll likely get a whopping. Ma will swear blind I've been playing tag with the boys in town again.' He kicked the bay mare into a steady trot and waved goodbye.

Pat thought about the saloon girl's statement; that this young boy was responsible for the death toll. 'Hold it, boy!' he shouted.

The boy checked his mount and turned in the saddle. 'What's up, mister?' His face was happy and full of joy. 'Do you want me to take you up to the ranch, to meet Ma? She'd be pleased to meet you all. We don't get many visitors up there.'

Pat was in a quandary. The boy was likeable and homely, and much too young to have been involved in a shootout, let alone kill a top gunslinger like Kid Rio and his two buddies. Nah, it was a silly notion, thought Pat; the saloon girl must have been stressed. 'Forget it, sonny. You go get that parcel for your Ma. And don't you be late now, you hear!' Pat waved the smiling boy off.

'I won't, mister,' shouted the boy as he cantered down the trail. 'See you all!'

'*Adios*,' shouted Pat.

'Which way?' shrugged Pancho, holding out both hands.

'Home,' snapped Pat, 'we've wasted enough time, as it is.' He spurred his horse in the opposite direction to Martha's ranch. 'It's a long way home, men,' he shouted, 'let's move it.' As they rode along, his thoughts centred on retiring from the Pinkerton Agency. He had been on the trail of these three outlaws a long time. It had been tiring. When they arrive back at base, he would resign and find something else to do. With those ideas in his mind, he cast out all thoughts of the boy and what might have happened in the Alamo Saloon.

Having decided on the homeward trail, Pat would never know the house of horrors that would have awaited him, had he taken the path leading to the ranch, and the horrendous death that Martha had suffered at the hands of her own son. And he could never have guessed that in the near future, he would cross paths with the young boy again. As sheriff, Pat Garrett was destined to meet William H. Bonney, alias Billy the Kid, one more time.

When the posse had disappeared into the fading sunset, William dismounted his horse. He untied the blanket roll that was tied at the back of the saddle, and shook it lose. The gun belt dropped to the floor. He strapped it around his waist. Then with lightning reflexes he drew the gun, and holstered it. He was a man now – free from the cruel bitch who had reared him. His eyes narrowed and moistened as he relived the moment when he had killed his mother. But they were not tears of remorse or guilt; they were tears of bitter hatred.

For the first time in his life, he was at liberty do whatever he wanted. No one was ever going to whip him, starve him, or lock him away. Never again would he go hungry, do the chores, or be without money. This was a new beginning, and no one was going to tell him what to do, ever again. From now on, he would take whatever he wanted, and woe betide anyone who got in the way. Elated with feelings of freedom, he climbed onto his horse. He sat for a while as deadly plans flitted through his mind. The days of running errands for the surveyor and cleaning out horse muck at the blacksmith's for a few cents were over. He would go to the barn, pick out the best horse in the corral for his own, then he would take all the money from the safe in the surveyor's office.

But the first stop would be the Alamo Saloon, where everyone had sat and watched his father being murdered, and no one had tried to save him. Now it was their turn. He would teach them all a lesson. Malevolence bubbled over like a boiling cauldron and surpassed any other hatred that he had ever known. Evil thoughts festered inside his mind and found their expression in a shout of rage. 'No one's going to stop me now. *No one!* And if anyone tries, I'll kill them. I'll kill them all!'

He kicked the bay mare into action. The animal whinnied and reared on its hind legs. He kicked again, and the steed charged forward in a cloud of dust. With feverish thoughts of doling out death, he lashed out repeatedly with the reins. The horse stretched into a full gallop, taking Billy the Kid onward towards Hang Tree Falls – and revenge!

THE END

Wild West Obituaries

Age

1859 - 1881   21   **Billy the Kid:** shot dead by sheriff Pat Garret in a dark alleyway in Mexico.

1850 - 1908   57   **Pat Garret:** shot dead in an ambush. Killers - unknown?

1848 - 1889   40   **Belle Starr:** believed to have been shot dead by her son, or husband. With little proof, neither was found guilty.

1847 - 1882   34   **Jesse James:** shot in the back by Robert Newton Ford, a new member of the James Gang.

1862 - 1892   30   **Robert Newton Ford:** shot to death in his temporary tent saloon in Colorado.

1844 - 1916   72   **Cole Younger:** a member of the Jesse James gang. Died of natural causes.

1837 - 1876   39   **Wild Bill Hickok:** was shot in the back whilst playing cards in a saloon. Killer - Jack McCall.

1852 - 1877   24   **Jack McCall:** execution - hanged for Wild Bill Hickok's murder.

1851 - 1887   36   **Doc Holiday:** died of tuberculosis.

1851 - 1878   27   **Sam Bass:** shot and killed by a Texas Ranger.

1845 - 1882   36 **Curly Bill:** reputedly killed by Wyatt Earp

1850 - 1882   32 **Johnny Ringo:** reputedly killed by Doc Holiday

1853 - 1895   42 **Wes Hardin:** shot in the back of the head by an outlaw, whilst playing dice in a saloon.

1848 - 1929   80 **Wyatt Earp**: died at home of chronic cystitis.

Lightning Source UK Ltd.
Milton Keynes UK
UKHW040635021020
370915UK00001B/202